CONTESTATORY CUBAN SHORT STORY OF THE REVOLUTION

José B. Alvarez IV

University Press of America,® Inc.
Lanham · New York · Oxford

Copyright © 2002 by
University Press of America,® Inc.
4720 Boston Way
Lanham, Maryland 20706
UPA Acquisitions Department (301) 459-3366

12 Hid's Copse Rd.
Cumnor Hill, Oxford OX2 9JJ

All rights reserved
Printed in the United States of America
British Library Cataloging in Publication Information Available

ISBN 0-7618-2344-1 (paperback : alk. ppr.)

∞™ The paper used in this publication meets the minimum
requirements of American National Standard for Information
Sciences—Permanence of Paper for Printed Library Materials,
ANSI Z39.48—1984

Para
El Negro y Raquel Alvarez
mis padres
Irene Alessandra Alvarez
mi retoño.

CONTENTS

PROLOGUE vii

ACKNOWLEDGMENTS xiii

Chapter One
    Cuban Writing: Historic and Cultural Context 1

Chapter Two
    Cuban Short Story: A Pendulum Movement 17

Chapter Three
    The Cuban Short Story of the *Novísimos* 41

Chapter Four
    The Dialectics of Homoeroticism in Cuban Narrative ... 71

APPENDIX
    Round Table with Four Cuban Intellectuals:
    "Culture of the Cuban Revolution —
    a Fluctuating Movement" 105

WORKS CITED 133

Prologue

Cuban literature continues to be one of the most intriguing areas of Latin American cultural production, more than anything else because of the central role Cuba plays in the consciousness of the continent and the research this fact has generated. Cuba and its socialist experience, Cuba and the embargo, Cuba and Cubans both inside and outside the country all constitute, far and away, one of the most prominent axis of the analytical awareness of Latin American history for almost fifty years. It is not so much a matter of one's interest in other areas and regions of Latin America, because the "Cuban case" always returns to intrude in one's consciousness as an unalterable return to a phenomenon that leaves its mark on all intellectual activity with regard to Latin America.

The consequence of such an intrusion—which is as much moral and it is social, as much political as it is cultural—is that Cuban culture has been privileged in research on Latin America, bringing together no only the attention of an impressive undertaking of Cuban specialists, but also because specialists of other countries must concern themselves, sooner or later, with aspects of Cuba's cultural production. The result is an exemplary bibliographic coverage not enjoyed, to go no farther than the rest of the Caribbean—by either Puerto Rican or Dominican culture. Moreover, besides Cuba's notable scholars, Cuban production has earned for itself the attention of some of the most respected names in Latin America, Europe, and the United States. Without a doubt, we are speaking of a research area that has been well heeded, well mined, and singularly represented in the quality of the publications it has generated.

Nevertheless, as much as attention has been devoted to outstanding sectors of Cuban production such as narrative, poetry, and theater, it is important to note that, with the exception of very fragmentary studies, there exist no evaluations of filmmaking as a whole (one of the most significant dimensions of contemporary Cuban cultural production, one that has attracted exceptional international attention), the sociopolitical essay and the essay of ideas, nor the short story.

The importance of Álvarez's book is that it proposes to remedy this lack with regard to the short story (and he is currently at work on a monograph devoted to the ideological analysis of Cuban filmmaking). Thus, this study is significant because it is centered on a genre that has not been adequately examined. That it has not is curious indeed, since the short story lends itself in a certain way to wide distribution, because it can be included, in terms of complete texts, in newspapers and journals, which is not possible in the case of theater or the novel, except when the latter are represented by fragments.

Nevertheless, the short story is a "difficult" genre because its limited extension, as Borges was fond of noting, imposes a synthesis and an expressive intensity that alienates the consumer from the sort of inattentive reading the novel often allows for. The result is that the short story, to a great extent, never ceases to be a marginal production.

It is precisely for this reason that Álvarez undertakes his study of the short story. The originality of the resulting monograph, nevertheless, is not simply the fact that he has provided a panoramic overview of the genre, but that he has chosen to approach it with the rigor of contemporary cultural studies, which in turn involves the theoretical imperative of examining cultural production as an ideological reading of the sociopolitical context in which it occurs and in which it is distributed, consumed, and interpreted. As a response to the question as to what degree the contemporary Cuban short story participates in the networks of cultural production in Cuba during the past decades, Álvarez offers a detailed analysis of principal texts and the outlines of their narrative discourse. It is at this juncture impossible to continue to conceive of literature as a sort of "mirror" of sociopolitical circumstances, and much less as a direct and facile response—whether favorable or negative—of a revolutionary process. Rather, what we have is a production that responds, in different dimensions and in very complex ways that are never reducible to transparent interpretations, to the accumulated weight of Cuban history, as much in its contemporary projections as in its full chronological sweep.

This survey, along one of its axes, does adhere to chronologically historical parameters, in the sense that it is grounded in the period immediately prior to the Revolution and traces the enormous modifications in narrative formats that are the consequence of the equally enormous changes in Cuban society since 1959, in the formation of writers and their reading public, in publishing and distributing formats for literature and—above all else—in the sociocultural contexts in which this production is interpreted and analyzed. The proper complement for this survey is the contextualization—one that cannot be definitive, because it can only exist in terms of some other dynamic of assessment—offered by the appendix of interviews with intellectuals and cultural producers, many of whom have not yet had the opportunity to have their positions of self-analysis and reflection represented by creditable critical conversation prior to this project, which Álvarez undertook on various trips to Cuba during the final years of the 1990s.

One of the greatest merits of this study, aside from the quality of its scope and the analytical rigor with which it is executed, is that it concerns itself with the homoerotic dimension of the short story. The fact that there has been a resurgence of a visible homoerotic culture in Cuba (one needs to avoid using both the medico-juridical term "homosexual" and the postmodern late capitalist one of "gay" with reference to the parameters of the desire among men in Cuba) is one of the most notable happenings of the past decade, patching over once and for all the lamentable parenthesis of the morality campaigns of previous years and the tragic experience of the UMAP concentration camps (a phenomenon lamentably recycled in the North American consciousness—much of which is always ready instantly to deplore post-revolutionary Cuba—by Julian Schnabel's *Before Night Falls*, based on Reinaldo Arenas's autobiography; the ideological problem here is that Schanbel's film, among other serious defects, is quick to repeat Arenas's denouncements of his persecutions for being queer, but it attenuates to the point of elimination everything Arenas had to say about the United States and Cubans residing in the United States, thereby reinforcing solely the violations of sexual rights that took place in Cuba up to the 1980s).

Cuba has always enjoyed a particularly open culture regarding the expressions of sensuality and sexuality, and it is a culture in which the display of the feminine body is accompanied by the exhibition of the male body in ways that might border on the indecent in other Latin American or European societies, not to mention in the U.S., which believes itself to be more "sober and reserved" in general than Cuba is thought to be. This does not mean that Cuban society is in any way more integrally homoerotic than other societies, but rather that it has traditionally permitted more visibility for phenomena that might be considered as signs of a greater visibility of sexualities that are universal and eternal among humankind. That these signs might, at some point, have come to constitute part of the attention of a project of social and moral cleansing is one thing; that they continued to exist, veiled or closeted, manifest or touted, in different periods of Cuban society is quite something different.

As far as literature—and the short story in particular—is concerned, it is necessary to distinguish between that production that concerns itself directly or indirectly with homoeroticism (however the latter is understood and whatever beliefs about it are held) and those texts in which the reading/interpretive process is able to discern the manifestation of considerations, situations, attitudes and behaviors that, in some way, are resistant to the imperative of compulsive heterosexuality. It is a well established principle in contemporary theorizing regarding cultural production that the phenomenon of meaning is difficult to contain in the operations of discourse and that the interpretation of a text is something that always gets away from both the author and the reader, allowing, in this way, all sorts of approaches to what is "really" going on in the semiotic universe of the text.

The foregoing does not in any way pretend to legitimate fanciful or tendentious readings of cultural production (as much as these might, from some point of view, be as valid as any others). Rather, it ought to serve more to underscore how—especially in moments in which a cultural production written within a context of organized censorship—a text may make use of many procedures to express that which cannot be named, procedures that it is the critical reader's obligation to untangle and elucidate. And the homoerotic in our societies—and in particular in the early years of the Cuban Revolution, as mentioned above—undeniably belongs to the category of that which cannot be named for the way in which it goes against the grain of the patriarchy that sustains the traditional oligarchy and, curiously, for the way in which it also challenges the concept of the "New Man" that synthesizes one ideological branch of the first stage of the 1959 Revolution.

As is well known, Senel Paz's famous story, "El lobo, el bosque y el hombre nuevo," signaled an important change in attitudes, which can be seen in particular in the film version of the story directed by Tomás Gutiérrez Alea, *Fresa y chocolate*, which premiered in late 1993 and has come to be possibly one of the most viewed Cuban films since then. Now that political and economic circumstances in Cuba no longer allow for much concern over sexual morality—something that has undeniably stimulated changes in to how people view homoeroticism—it is not surprising that there has been an increasing bibliography on the subject, a fact that emerges very emphatically in the chapter Álvarez devotes in his study to it.

Solid in its use of pertinent theoretical bibliography, especially as regards to cultural studies, and enriched by a large array of examined material, Álvarez's book constitutes an important contribution to research on Cuban cultural production under the shadow of the Revolution and its projections throughout subsequent decades.

David William Foster
Arizona State University

ACKNOWLEDGMENTS

The research for this study was made possible by various grants programs of the University of Georgia. The Center for Humanities and Arts, and the Graduate College provided generous monetary support that made possible my many research stays in Cuba. Also, the Department of Romance Languages has allow me to teach many courses in my specialization that provided the sounding board for the material presented in this book

I wish to acknowledge the contribution to my research that many people have made over the years and their eternal friendship. First and foremost, I am grateful to David William Foster, teacher and friend who ten years ago opened his enthusiasm and knowledge to me at Arizona State University. Carmen Chaves Tesser became my mentor and friend upon my arrival at the University of Georgia. She graciously and unselfishly put to work her expertise and translated from the original Spanish chapters 1, 2 and 3 of this book. Chapter 4 was translated by my great friend and Spanish film scholar Christina Buckley of Furman University, and the roundtable by Laurie Allen Frederik, friend and fellow Cubanist scholar. To all three I express my infinite gratitude. In Cuba many people have contributed to my research over the years, especially: Juan Nicolás Padrón, Ricardo Hernández, Jorge Domingo, and Salvador Redonet. My students at the University of Georgia have always enriched me with their intelligence and boundless inquisitiveness about Cuba, especially: Diego del Pozo, Elena Adell, Mónica Ruiz-Meléndez, Spencer Willbanks, Catherine Simpson, and Joe Goldstein. Lastly, Daniela Melis has been my greatest supporter from film to theater with the stop overs in Spain and Italy, *contigo desde la escalera*....

CHAPTER 1

CUBAN WRITING:
HISTORIC AND CULTURAL CONTEXT

INTRODUCTION

The mere act of writing or enunciating the name of the largest of the Antilles incites multiple reactions, some betraying an intellectual sphere, provoked by fanaticism of one kind or another. The project of writing a book about the evolution of the Cuban short story from 1959 to the early 1990s transcend's a discussion of literary texts and sends one toward a highly political-ideological discourse that will encounter both support as well as strong opposition.

To be able to analyze the contestatory elements in Cuban short stories, as I propose to do, it is important to contextualize this thematic with an explanatory summary that will point to the trajectory undertaken by the so called literature of the Revolution.

The study of Cuban narrative produced on the island after the triumph of the 1959 revolution is nothing new. For example, excellent comprehensive works by scholars such as Seymour Menton, *Prose Fiction of the Cuban Revolution* (1975); Ernesto Méndez y Soto, *Panorama de la novela cubana de la revolución 1959-1970* (1977); Rogelio Rodríguez Coronel, *Novela de la revolución y otros temas* (1983); and Armando Pereira, *Novela de la revolución cubana* (1960-1990) all present panoramic studies about the abundance of Cuban novels written between 1959 and

1990. These studies select and analyze a group of novels and offer a global vision of the themes treated in them.

SUCCESSES

No one can deny the great positive influence that the Cuban Revolution had on the Latin American political consciousness and on the cultural thought of the entire Third World during the decade of the sixties. A few months after the guerrilla triumph, Haydee Santamaría founded, under governmental auspices, Casa de las Américas (1959), a cultural center that provides space to Latin American writers who previously lacked access to publishing houses due to economic or political reasons. Consequently, Casa de las Américas revolutionized literary publishing mechanisms on the continent, establishing, for example, large volume editions without any cost to the author and with prices that were affordable for the public. Moreover, the center established literary prizes in different genres opening participation to all Latin Americans writers. In literary circles, there was an almost instant flourishing of journals and literary supplements as well as a great dissemination of young poets, narrators, and essayists. Likewise, the journal *Casa de las Américas*, founded in 1960 by Santamaría and today under the direction of Roberto Fernández Retamar, established itself in the 1960s as the artistic vanguard of the Latin American left where renowned intellectuals from throughout the world collaborated with high quality articles giving the journal a well deserved prestige. At the same time, other publishing outlets appeared, such as *El caimán barbudo* (1966-89, 1996-present), initially under the direction of Jesús Díaz; *Lunes* (1950-61), edited until its closing by Guillermo Cabrera Infante; and *Revolución* (1959-1965). Cuban cultural politics also had an impact at the international level, since it encouraged foreign writers, painters and theoreticians to further their professional development, university studies or exploration of their intellectual abilities within the cultural institutions of the Island without having to worry about the problems presented to people of lower incomes by a capitalist society. Generous scholarships that covered enrollment, food, lodging and personal expenses were available to anyone who applied for them, mostly intellectuals from Latin America and Africa.

The cultural mechanisms and institutions from the Island under the state budget have catapulted to an international sphere a large number of writers from different generations or groups who were considered loyal to the Revolution's ideology. For the last four decades, narrators and poets of the various generations and literary promotions, such as Nicolás Guillén, Roberto Fernández Retamar, Miguel Barnet, Mirta Aguirre, Nancy Morejón, Lisandro Otero, Jesús Díaz, Abel Prieto, Senel Paz, Raúl Hernández Novás, Jorge Luis Hernández, Arturo Arango, Leonardo Padura Fuentes, have taken advantage of an educational, cultural, and editorial policy that has never been within reach of the majority of writers from other Latin American countries. Nevertheless, there exists a group of writers who are marginalized at the national level, and therefore, also at the international level[1] that has not had the opportunity to publish in Cuba; in the best of cases, their works have seen a few, very limited Cuban editions, lacking the appropriate and necessary public exposure.

In this group, three great writers from two different generations are worth noting: José Lezama Lima (1910-76), Virgilio Piñera (1912-79) and Reinaldo Arenas (1943-90). Lezama Lima was a poet, essayist, and fiction writer who, at the triumph of the Revolution was already internationally recognized for his work and for the editorship of the then defunct *Orígenes* (1944-56); his novel

---

1. Until 1994, publication of manuscripts abroad was prohibited without proper government authorization (Marín 14, Castro "Fidel en el V Congreso de la UNEAC" 4-5). Among others, Reinaldo Arenas and Roberto Luque Escalona were sanctioned for publishing abroad. The later was expelled from the University of Havana, where he worked in the journal *Economía y desarrollo,* for publishing the book *Fidel el juicio de la historia (1990)* in Mexico.

Paradiso (1966) was the object of a very limited edition (4,000 copies) without hardly any publicity. When the novel went out of print, it was not republished in Cuba until the decade of the 80's, several years after the author's death. From its initial publication, this great universal literary work encountered a strong opposition from the official cultural circles, since it was considered a homoerotic narrative not in accordance with the new cultural policy[2] that the State tried to promote through mandate. In the case of Reinaldo Arenas, his second novel *El mundo alucinante, una novela de aventuras (1969)* earned an honorific mention in the Casa de las Américas literary prize competition in 1966. Nevertheless, in spite of also receiving a prize in France, this work was never published in Cuba because it did not exalt the success of the Revolution; the official response was to say that it was not published due to a paper shortage in the country.[3]

---

2. The cultural policy of the new Cuban government had as an objective the formation of a New Man; this movement called for the development of a new generation of individuals whose social consciousness would be above the interests of the capitalist societies (Oppenheimer 270). It is important to mention that this concept is commonly attributed to Che Guevara; nevertheless, much before this time, the Soviets spoke of the same phenomenon, calling for the "destruction of the old customs" (Gorki 46). Of course, the imperative to create a new individual does not originate with either the Cubans or the Russians; this type of transformation can be found in such diverse sources as Biblical Christianity and Nietszchean Humanism, among others.

3. During one of my trips to Cuba in the early 90s, I confirmed that groups of many generations of university students, Cuban literature students that is, not only are unfamiliar with the work of Reinaldo Arenas, but have never heard of him. It must be said that his first novel, *Celestino antes del alba,* won a First Mention Award at the 1965 Cirilo Villaverde National Competition and was published by UNEAC in 1967. This will be the only one of Arena's novels that would be published in Cuba. In the case of Lezama Lima, the issue is not as critical, but similar. As an example, see the attention paid to the poet in the film *Fresa y chocolate* (1993) where in a humorous fashion, we realize the slight dissemination

Due to nationalization and state appropriation of all private property in 1968, publishing houses became controlled by state institutions, creating an atmosphere of "silent censorship" that afterwards—for the literary survival of the writer—would become self-censorship, as in the case of Virgilio Piñera whom we discuss in chapter four. Those who held the highly political position of "Editor" had, until the early 1990s, the power of deciding who and how many works will be published. Moreover, in Cuba, from 1959, the most powerful intellectuals were those who became politicians and, following official mandates, used criteria solely restricted to politics (in the most vulgar sense of the word) to judge literary activity and production. Overnight a literary or artistic career could fall into disgrace for political reasons. The case that received the most international attention (perhaps because from that moment on many foreign intellectuals[4] became aware of the other Cuban cultural reality and consequently stopped supporting the Revolution), was that of Heberto Padilla (1932-2000), who in 1971 was taken to prison after having read, in the Cuban Writers and Artists Union (UNEAC), some poems from his book, *Provocaciones* (1973).

---

and recognition that the Master received after the publication of *Paradiso* (1966). It must be mentioned that from the middle of the 1980s, the cultural policy has been to recover Lezama Lima, Virgilio Piñera, Octavio Smith, Calvert Casey, and many others who during their lives suffered discrimination due to their ideological stance. In 1993, the Letras Cubanas publishing house published three books written by Lezama Lima.

4. Signed by well known foreign intellectuals (among them Jean Paul Sartre, Mario Vargas Llosa and Carlos Fuentes) two letters were sent directly to Fidel Castro condemning the treatment given to Padilla. The Peruvian writer resigned in 1971 from the Committee for Collaboration of the Casa de las Américas in a letter directed to Haydee Santamaría dated April 5. Santamaría's response was to label him a "colonized writer, not appreciative of our peoples" (17).

By that time, Padilla had already been strongly criticized by several intellectual sectors,[5] verbally as well as in writing, for having participated with his collection of poems, *Fuera de juego* (1968) in the poetry contest sponsored by the UNEAC in 1968, and winning it. This book, like the work, *Los siete contra Tebas* (1968) by Antón Arrufat (1935-), was published under protest by Ediciones Unión with a note from the Executive Committee of the UNEAC expressing its disagreement with the award since it considered the books "ideologically contrary to the Revolution" (7). Although Padilla is the best known of the intellectuals marginalized for themes broached in their literary production and for wanting to practice their right to a different ideology, there are many others that are mostly unknown internationally: Manuel Ballagas, René Ariza, Eduardo Heras León, Rafael Saumell, Ariel Hidlago, Luis Ruiz, Gastón Hernández Martínez, Armando Valladares, María Elena Cruz Varela. The different generations represented in these authors confirm that the political-ideological dissidence expressed through literature has been present from the beginning of the revolution and that through the contestatory texts we may attain a view—a history, let us say—different from the one that has been disseminated through he official means.

From 1976, with the creation of the Ministry of Culture under the direction of Armando Hart Dávalos (1930),[6] and with the decentralization of the publishing groups, there came about a moderate opening through which each publishing house could employ its own individual advisory boards, with relative powers,

---

5. An article signed by "Leopoldo Avila" (a pseudonym used by Luis Pavón and four other intellectuals) appeared in *Verde olivo* accusing Padilla of using *Fuera de juego* to provoke UNEAC, to raise falsehoods and to work for Imperialism. Avila said: "although he believes himself to be out of the game, the rules of the Revolution are stated" ("Las provocaciones de" 18).

6. Armando Hart was Minister of Culture of Cuba from 1976 to 1997 when the writer Abel Prieto, then president of UNEAC, was appointed as his replacement.

to choose what would be published. This step meant that, up to a point, there was a separation between aesthetics and politics. Cuban literature began to move slowly toward a dose of criticism more in line with the reality that was being described, provided that there was no direct allusion to those who were on the top political stratus. Nevertheless, censorship and repression still exist today.

CULTURAL-LITERARY ANTECEDENTS

The revolutionary government created the first cultural organization on March 24, 1959, three months after the triumph of the Revolution. Through law # 169, the Cuban Film Institute (Instituto Cubano de Arte en Industria Cinematográficas ICAIC) was established and two years later the poet Nicolás Guillén founded the UNEAC. Among others, the objectives and goals of both institutions can be summarized by the following ideological parameters outlined in the law that created ICAIC:

> Cinema must embody a calling to consciousness and must contribute to abolishing ignorance, to solving problems, to formulating solutions, and it should pose dramatically and contemporaneously the great conflicts between man and humanity [...]. Cinema constitutes, by virtue of its characteristics, an instrument of opinion and formation of individual and collective consciousness and can make deeper and more transparent the revolutionary spirit and help to sustain its creative spirit. (*Diez años de cine cubano* 8)

If we add to these objectives the controversial Castrist maxim: "Within the Revolution everything; outside the Revolution, nothing,"[7] we see that what was presented by the ICAIC is an

---

7. This quotation has become famous and still motivates discussion about its meaning. It is taken from a presentation by Fidel Castro in June of 1961 in the National Library before a number of intellectuals

explicit governmental proposal of the ideological norm to be followed by all artists, writers, and filmmakers who want to work in the Island. The ICAIC, as well as the UNEAC, display an ideological agenda for indoctrinating the population through art and, as will be seen later, these are goals demanded by the Soviet Leninist-Stalinist thought. This indoctrination is evident in some of the titles of early published novels, *Mañana es 26* (1960), by Hilda Perera Soto; *Maestra voluntaria* (1962) by Daura Olema García; *Concentración pública* (1964) by Paul González Cascarro; *Girón en la memoria* (1971) by Víctor Casaus; and films and documentaries such as *Patria o muerte (1960),* by Julio García Espinosa; *De la tiranía a la libertad, Me hice maestro(1961),* by Jorge Fraga, *Las aventuras de Juan Quin Quin* (1967) by Julio García Espinosa, *Hasta la victoria siempre* (1967) by Santiago Alvarez, *Lucía* (1968) by Humberto Solás; *Memorias del subdesarrollo* (1968) by Tomás Gutiérrez Alea; *La primera carga del machete* (1969) by Manuel Octavio Gómez, all tracing the new society that the Revolution wanted to develop in Cuba during the first decade in power.

To contextualize our proposal with a literary work, we can refer to the novel *Volunteer Teacher* (1962) by Olema García. Upon reading this work, it becomes explicit that the purpose of the narrative is to disseminate a particular ideology, as it praises uniformity, comradeship, communal sacrifice and respect to officialdom. That is to say, the novel states those ideological parameters under which one must live in the recently installed socialist state. At the same time, the novel contrasts the living conditions of the people during the Batista government and those of the new

---

summoned there: "I believe that this is quite clear... What are the rights of revolutionary writers and artists? Within the Revolution, everything; against the Revolution no rights" (cited in Avila, "Sobre algunas" 15). In the same presentation cited by Avila, Castro also says, "A Revolution is a historical process [...] a Revolution is not, nor can it be, the work of capriciousness or of the wish of any man [...] the Revolution can only be the work of necessity and the wish of the people" (16).

socialist regime. All these are recurring themes in the literature of the first fifteen years of the revolution. As for the filmic production, we could mention films such as *Lucía* (1968) or *Memories of Underdevelopment* (1968)—in which the concept of the new revolutionary man and woman is presented as the norm of all good citizens.

During the first decade of the Revolution, films, works of theater, plastic arts or other cultural spaces in the country, included—to a greater or lesser degree—a certain dose of criticism. On the other hand, mass distribution of magazines and newspapers seen in the streets from 1959 carried very reasonable prices and inspiring patriotic titles—such as *Granma, Juventud rebelde, Trabajadores, Verde olivo*—and constantly praised the great successes of the revolution, contained pleas for communal and individual sacrifice, attacked imperialism, exalted at all costs the words of the Comrade/Commander Fidel and, most importantly, never contained criticism directed at him or the politburo.[8]

THE PRESENT STUDY

The goal of the present study is twofold. First, I propose to analyze the contestatory project[9] that can be found in texts

---

8. It should be noted that nowadays, even when the situation in the country is extremely critical, newspapers that are still lucky enough to be in the streets sporadically, television and radio news as well as other means of social communication, continue to exalt the success of the Revolution and justify the austere official methods. Suffice it to say that the state control and the censorship of these means of communication are still alive.

9. The technique used depends on the date in which the work is produced, experiencing the period of greatest opening with the works written since the mid 1980s. Works like "¿Por qué llora Leslie Caron?" (1987) by Roberto Urías, "*El lobo, el bosque y el hombe nuevo*" (1990) by Senel Paz, and "Dorado mundo" (1993) by Francisco López Sacha, would have never been published in the 1970s, since they directly reflect

produced from 1959 on; second, and as an inevitable result of the first goal, I plan to bring forth another history of revolutionary Cuba, vis-à-vis the official story. Therefore, through critical rereading, I will reach conclusions that will be, in many cases, in direct opposition to the vision that the Cuban official story has tried to project to the world. This implies that through textual analysis, we will realize that in post-revolutionary Cuba there is and has been prostitution, homosexuality, indiscriminate repression of citizens, racial, sexual, and gender discrimination, privileged classes, corruption, false liberty and other so called evils attributed repeatedly to capitalism and with much effort hidden by Castro's government, but that are, nonetheless, realities that affect any present day society. As a result, I will show that important segments of the cultural production of the Island have not ignored the reality that surrounds, and occasionally subjugates, the artist himself.

To facilitate the organization of the study, and according to historical issues that mold cultural production and its relation with the censorship/resistance dialectic in Cuba, I have divided the study into four chapters and two appendixes with two separate interviews. The second chapter focuses on the better known writers of three distinct postrevolutionary generations. The third chapter analyzes the production of the *Novísimos* and in the fourth one, Cuban homoerotic narrative in the twentieth century is the focus.

It should be noted that when the revolutionary government of Cuba declared itself to be Marxist (Marxist-Leninist, Socialist-Communist, Martian-Nationalist are terms that change in the official discourse according to the historical period) it comes into counter position to the official culture unilaterally established, one of *resistance* with the pretension of combating ideological control that the State shows in its authoritarian practices. The authoritarian

---

a critical view of Cuban society, with its nepotism, official corruption, black market or other themes that are considered taboo, such as homosexuality.

exercise of power by the government is incongruous with the Marxist dicta of liberation; the ostensible goals of a socialist system installed precisely to free the people are undermined by the presence of the intelligentsia, who lived under political-economic oppression of a military dictatorship and by the degeneration of capitalism that controlled and subjugated the population.

Maxims such as "literature must be part of the common cause of the proletariat" (Lenin 56); "writers are the engineers of the soul" (Stalin; cited in Ruhle 232) and "within the Revolution everything; outside the Revolution, nothing" (Castro; cited in Avila 16), give a sense of liberty to creativity and to free expression that every artist has the right to exercise under a Marxist practice, using coercion—toward the writer, film maker, composer—to adjust to ideological parameters with political and not aesthetic parameters that do not tolerate but sanction artistic expressions in other latitudes. As a point of contrast to the maxims cited, we seek support in the words of León Trotsky: "it is very true that one cannot always go by the principles of Marxism in deciding whether to reject or accept a work of art. A work of art should, in the first place, be judged by its own law, that is, by the law of art" (73), a principle not accepted in Cuba, especially after the National Education and Culture Congress in 1971.

As a principle,[10] and with respect to Cuba, I understand the general concept of censorship as the function of power— authoritarian or totalitarian in the most extreme case—that an official tribunal or public authority exercises, to "control the ideological content of information, ideas, graphic or dramatic representations destined to reach the public through the many forms of social communication" (Di Tella 69). Even though it is difficult to define the term "resistance culture" in this study, I use it to mean a

---

10. I say "as a principle," since the concept of censorship comes in different types, such as silent censorship, self-censorship, previous or after-the-fact censorship, moral censorship, depending on different historical periods.

movement in the hands of individuals or sectors in the Cuban culture that react against the political, ideological and cultural parameters established unilaterally from the centers of power, that is, the Political Bureau, the Ministry of Culture, UNEAC, or ICAIC. It should be noted that this phenomenon is not limited to the post-revolutionary period, but that we can trace it through Cuban history, initially in the final independentist movements of the end of the nineteenth century and continuing until the arrival of the insurrectional fights against the Batista dictatorship in the 1950s.

In this study, I will use the framework presented by Barbara Harlow in *Resistance Literature* (1987), keeping in mind that the author did not study the Cuban case and that her emphasis is on resistance literature produced by writers who belong to movements of national liberation in Third World countries who suffer the oppression of imperialism, colonialism, or rightist military dictatorships. Her model studies the literature written in South Africa, Nicaragua, El Salvador, Bolivia, Mozambique, Kenya and Palestine.

Harlow argues that the term *resistance* was used for the first time, with reference to literature, by the Palestine writer and critic Ghassan Kanafani in his study *Literature of Resistance in Occupied Palestine: 1948-1966*. Here the critic divides resistance literature into two categories, according to the condition under which they were written: under occupation and in exile, and at the same time, he underscores that because of these conditions, the literary camp converts itself into "an arena of struggle" (Harlow 2). That is to say, cultural resistance begins to be part of the liberation fight of one class, one group, one ideal that rises against the cultural production of the hegemonic ideology:

> Resistance literature calls attention to itself, and to literature in general, as a political and politicized activity. The literature of resistance sees itself furthermore as immediately and directly involved in a struggle against ascendant or dominant forms of ideological and cultural production. (Harlow 28-29)

The artistic production of the Cuban cultural resistance is an instrument that facilitates the revision of history; that is, resistance literature gives way to the diffusion of another history and it proposes its own history. I agree with Barbara Harlow when she affirms that the poets and narrators that resist cultural hegemony "seek to redefine through their [writing] the possibilities of a new, revised social order" (Harlow 50). There remains a last consideration to be contemplated with respect to this point. In resistance literature, produced in the heart of an autocratic regimen where censorship is an instrument of silence, the resistance writer is surrounded in what Humberto Eco calls "semiotic guerilla warfare" and therefore "one can trace a *tactic* of decoding where the message as expression form does not change but the addressee rediscovers his *freedom of decoding*" (150). The last consequences are that the writer and the reader (co)challenge the existing hegemonic order.

Terry Eagleton contemplates in his text, *Criticism and Ideology* (1976), that literature "constitutes the most revealing mode of experiential access to ideology available, more immediate than science [Marxist science] and more coherent than live experience," and at the same time, he argues that the literary text is not necessarily an exclusive representation of the dominant ideology. I agree with Eagleton in his view that the work of the critic is threefold: 1) to situate himself outside of the text and the ideology that it presents; 2) to see the text as an "open" entity, and 3) to go beyond the obvious and in so doing decode "its hidden knowledge" (cited in De Bruyn 301). This is the goal of the present study: to deconstruct the texts to be able to trace new historical parameters that may reveal "the truth during times of oppression" (Rama 524), that is, to (re)narrate or catch a glimpse of what has happened in Cuba during the Revolution.

CORPUS

This work focuses on the short story and homoerotic narrative written and published in Cuba after 1959. As far as the short story,

I dedicate two chapters to the study of the evolution of the genre from the works published in 1959 to those written in the early 1990s on the Island by those young people that Salvador Redonet has called the *Novísimos*.[11] In the chapter in which I focus on the homoerotic Cuban writing, there is a need to provide a historical background which brings my discussion back to the texts, *Angel de Sodoma* (1927) by Alfonso Hernández Catá, and *Hombres sin mujer* (1938) by Carlos Montenegro. I then focus on chapter eight of *Paradiso* (1966) and short stories published in the 1980s and early 1990s.

A large portion of the written corpus that I am studying has been published in national journals such as *La gaceta de Cuba* and *Letras cubanas*. It is lamentable that the paper shortage contributed to the small dissemination of new literary values. *Letras cubanas* was in the vanguard in promoting the *Novísimos*, beginning with issue number 9 (1988 until the early 1990's when it went out of print)—a fact not seen in other contemporary publications. Furthermore, journals such as *El caimán barbudo* (1966-85, 1996-present) completely disappeared, were not published for many years, or had a very limited circulation. Others were very sectary as has been the case with the journal *Casa de las Américas*.

I have been able to find out who has been writing on the Island during the last decade after researching in Cuba since 1989 and thanks to personal interviews with different Cuban writers and critics. Among others, I have spoken with Juan Nicolás Padrón, Salvador Redonet, Jorge Domingo, Ricardo Hernández, Eduardo Heras León, Miguel Barnet, Francisco López Sacha, Senel Paz, Amado del Pino and Elizabeth Díaz—writers, critics, editors—all who have been a vital source of information otherwise impossible to find outside of Cuba. As such, I have included in the appendix

---

11. In an interview conducted in June of 1995, the Cuban professor and critic, Salvador Redonet, said that the *Novísimos* encompass all those writers born between 1959 and 1972 (see appendix).

a very useful source of information: a round table with five leading Cuban intellectuals.

The primary objective of this study is to explore and analyze the evolution of the contestatory element in the Cuban short narrative that emerges as a consequence of the censorship-resistance dialectic. Therefore, in addition to discussing the written texts, in some cases I will take some examples from films, songs, humor and other elements that comprise the rich field of Cuban popular culture—an aspect that presents more difficulties in terms of control and censorship due to its orality—to intervene in the historical revision that I am suggesting.

I propose that there are some historical moments that bring about a contestatory artistic-cultural production after 1959 and that these moments reflect the censorship-resistance dialectic: the triumph of the Revolution (1959), the first wave of exiles (1959-61), the awards and official reaction toward *Fuera de juego* and *Los siete contra Tebas* (1968), The Congress of Education and Culture (1971), the Padilla Case (1971), the sanction of Eduardo Heras León after the publication of *Los pasos en la hierba* (1971), the creation of the Ministry of Culture (1976), the Cuban participation in the wars in Angola and Ethiopia (1978), the Mariel exodus (1980), the fall of the socialist block countries (1989), the international award given to the short story *El lobo, el bosque y el hombre nuevo* by Senel Paz (1990), and finally, the extraordinary success in Cuba and in the rest of the world of the film *Fresa y chocolate* (1993) by Tomás Gutiérrez Alea and Juan Carlos Tabío.

CHAPTER 2

CUBAN SHORT STORY FROM 1959 TO 1990: A PENDULUM MOVEMENT

> A literature that does not capture the social environment in which it is realized, that does not dare to give back to this same society it own themes and fears, that does not warn in a timely fashion the threat of moral and social dangers, such a literature does not deserve to be called literature, it is a mere facade. (Alejandro Solzhenitzyn; cited in *Padilla* 5)

> Be careful with the easy demagoguery of demanding a literature accessible to everyone! (Julio Cortázar 13)

> The short story is paradoxically one of the narrative forms that is at the same time ancient and modern: it is the telling of more or less unitary anecdotes in its plot and short in its length—told orally or in writing. (Rosa María Alcalá 8)

INTRODUCTION

The task before me in this chapter is one that requires a rigorous coverage of narrative material that, besides being extensive, presents distinctive marked traits depending on the time of its production. My goal is to trace the evolution of the Cuban short story from 1959 to the texts written by Senel Paz (b. 1950) whom I take to be an icon of the penultimate generation of Cuban writers, those born between 1950 and 1958.[1] The chapter is divided according to historical dates, and after setting the parameters in which I discuss briefly the evolution of the Cuban short story before the Revolution, I proceed to analyze representative texts and authors within four chronological movements and divisions: 1959-65, 1966-70, 1971-76 and 1977 to the writings of Senel Paz's generation.

Within this framework, my objective is twofold. First, I plan to present a panorama of the four parts or narrative movements that cover the thirty-five years of the Cuban short story, underscoring those short stories and writers who epitomize their respective times. Second, I am obliged to contextualize this analysis with a discussion of the historical times, their predominant ideologies, and their respective milestones, that will allow me to demonstrate the reason for the themes and narrative forms that characterize each generation.

HISTORICAL PARAMETERS

Even though Cuba is better known as a country of "musicians and poets" as Juan Nicolás Padrón[2] observed in the first interview that we had in 1993, the Island also has a rich short story tradition that begins during the 1940s, a time of the first period of formal and thematic maturity of short narrative. These years were ones of affirmation and recognition for authors such as: Lydia Cabrera (1899-1991), Lino Novás Calvo (1905-79), Alejo Carpentier

---

1. In next chapter we will cover the literary production of the *Novísimos*.

2. Padrón states, "[The pattern] has always been marked by poetry in Cuba, since the nineteenth century [...] The rest is secondary, there can appear a surge of plastic arts during some moment, four or five novels, we have a little of everything, but fundamentally we are one of the peoples having more poets per square kilometer in the world" (Alvarez "Literatura cubana de los 80" 94).

(1904-80), Virgilio Piñera (1912-79), Félix Pita Rodríguez (b. 1901), Onelio Jorge Cardoso (b. 1914) and others from later generations. All of them succeeded in establishing themselves within Hispanic narrative in spite of the crushing literary domination of the generation of poets from *Orígenes* (1944-56) led by its editors José Lezama Lima (1910-76)[3] and José Rodríguez Feo (1920-95). The aesthetic ideas of this later group, universalist and bourgeois, ignored the sociopolitical reality in which the country was immersed—marked by the phenomenon of corruption, racial discrimination, military dictatorship, political persecutions, and poverty. In 1942, the "National Short Story Prize Alfonso Hernández Catá" was established. The prize was determined by an intellectually prestigious jury, and in later years would come to have two annual contests: one national and another one international. This recognition, together with the journals *Bohemia* (1910-) and *Carteles* (1919-60), brought about support and space for the cultivation of the short story by young writers[4] that began to publish under the influence of existentialism. Tired of the reiterated and old |*criollista* current |and anxious to put to practice experimental form (ruptures, expressive searches, various foreign influences), authors such as Onelio Jorge Caroso, Félix Pita Rodríguez, Antonio Ortega, Carlos Montenegro (1900-81), and Dora Alonso (1910-2001) distinguished themselves among the winners of the above mentioned prize. As they matured, the young writers who began to flourish during these years, became the same ones who published the first short stories that surfaced at the triumph of the Revolution in 1959: Guillermo Cabrera Infante (b.

---

3. *Orígenes* was not the first incursion by Lezama Lima in the leading of a literary journal. With poet Angel Gaztely, he had earlier founded *Nadie parecía* (1941-43), *Espuela de plata* (1938039) and the first to appear *Verbum* (1937) (Lozano 21).

4. We must mention the Spanish political exiles who arrived at the Island: Luis Amado Blanco, Miguel Millares Vázquez, Antonio Ortega, Emilio Palomo and Lino Novás Calvo.

1929), César Leante (b. 1928), Lisandro Otero (b. 1932) and Humberto Arenal (b. 1926), are among the most well known.

The Cuban short story seems to be guided by pendulum movements controlled by political-ideological factors more than by aesthetic reasons. Thus, it was in the second half of the 1960s (1966-70), the time that eventually came to be known as the *Quinquenio de Oro* ("Golden Quinquennium"), that one finds the literary production of Jesús Díaz (b. 1940), Norberto Fuentes (b. 1943), Eduardo Heras León (b. 1943), Antonio Benítez Rojo (b. 1931), all winners of national literary prizes and deserving of the praise received from international critics. These writers succeed in underscoring in their writing "a narrative of the epic and of the violence in which they combined in harmony themes, characters, anecdotes, and language, to conform to an individual aesthetic" (Padura 39).

With the arrival of a new decade and with its accompanying economic-political-ideological factors that affected the Island, Cuban short story production suffered a strong blow and was forced to submit to an unprecedented amount of censorship. It is not by caprice that the period 1971-76 has been christened as the *Quinquenio Gris* ("Gray Quinquennium") of Cuban literary production. Not until the end of the 1970s and the beginning of the 80s, with the creation of the Ministry of Culture (1976) and the convening of the Cuban Literature Colloquium (1981) does one witness certain changes in the Cuban cultural policy which permitted a formal delimitation between literature and politics, thereby allowing the production of Cuban short story to flourish again. I use the date of 1976 to point to the culmination of the Gray Quinquennium since it is on this date that the Ministry of Culture was created. Nevertheless, I agree with Salvador Redonet when he affirms that:

> I would say that there was a bad hour, or a very gray period between '71 and '75, but it is extended, less radically, between '76 and '82, since the changes the Ministry of Culture brought did not take effect right away.(Alvarez "Ruptura")

It is a fallacy to speak of the Revolution's short story as something homogenous. The only possible common characteristics are that they were written by Cuban narrators and between the years 1959 and the present. It is not even useful to establish a geographic demarcation since it is valid to argue that the short stories written in exile by authors such as Daína Chaviano (b. 1957) in Miami, Carlos Montaner (b. 1943) in Madrid, Cabrera Infante (b. 1929) in London, Zoé Valdés (b. 1959) in Paris or René Vázquez Díaz (b. 1952) in Sweden—a group which spans one geographical extreme to the other—are also short stories of the Revolution even though they are written from different ideological positions.

Therefore, the immediate task is to establish a typology for the Cuban short story of the Revolution written in Cuba. To do so, it is necessary to divide the thirty-five-year span into several chronological periods that will be individually analyzed with differing degrees of detail according to the needs demanded by the production of the particular time.[5]

THE INITIAL YEARS: 1959-65

To begin, one has to consider that Cuba was the first Hispano American country—and the only one with the exception of Nicaragua in 1979— where a popular revolution, within a framework of Marxist-Leninist doctrine, ousted a rightist military dictator, that had been installed, supported and subjected by the United States, and replaced it with a government that had the approval of the

---

5. It should be noted that since the Cuban short story production is so rich, we find few complex theoretical studies that analyze this narrative form as a whole. In 1967, Ambrosio Fornet published a critical study entitled *En blanco y negro,* and then not until the end of the 1970s does one find two essays evaluating the situation of the Cuban short story: "Rumbos de los más jóvenes cuentistas" (1979) written by Arturo Arango and "Panorama del cuento cubano" (1980) by Sergio Chaple (López Sacha "El cuento ante la crítica cubana" 23).

majority of the people. This ousting was not done through peaceful means. The long and bloody battles—that have their first international repercussion during the assault at the Moncada garrison in Santiago de Cuba on July 26, 1953—continued in the Sierra Maestra as well as in the urban zones until the dictator Batista fled from the country on January 1, 1959. The installation of the new revolutionary government brought to the country a period of relative calm that was interrupted by the failed invasion of Playa Girón (1961) and by the fights against counterrevolutionary guerrillas in the mountains of Escambray in the central part of Cuba between the years of 1960 and 1966. These years were marked by a violence that possessed several traits that affected almost the entire population. In the first place, the warlike violence—in the countryside as well as in the urban zones—brought guerrillas face to face with army troops and governmental police. On the other hand, there were vile acts—tortures, assassinations, rapes—carried out by the security institutions of the State. All these manifestations of violence plagued the life of Cubans for many years and necessarily will be featured in the Cuban short story of the next ten years.

At the triumph of the Revolution, different cultural spaces appear to support the development of Cuban literature. Publishing houses like Casa de las Américas, Ediciones R and El Puente, and journals and literary supplements such as *Lunes de revolución* (1959-61), *Unión* (1962-present), *Casa de las Américas* (1960-present), all open their pages to narratives previously banned for political and/or economic reasons. One example is the work of Guillermo Cabrera Infante, who in 1960 published the Cuban edition of *Así en la paz como en la guerra,* a book comprising: "short stories [and vignettes] written during the last ten years [1950-58]" (Cabrera 7). The fifteen vignettes, narrated in the past and in third person, are a clear representation of life (or death?) under the dictatorial tyranny of Batista: "I've only permitted myself—writes Cabrera Infante—slight alterations of reality, adapting the difficult (or simply sinister) life to literary necessities" (7). The protagonists involved in the tortures and assassinations are

"Joe, the client, the sailors, the black young man, Frank;" among them there are young and old, white, black and mulattoes, educated and illiterate, representing the myriad Cubans who suffered the vexations of the dictatorship. Mixed in are fourteen long stories in which the interpersonal violence of the 1950s is portrayed: poverty, prostitution, national gangsters, adultery, and racial discrimination. The stories collected in *Así en la paz como en la guerra,* like many of the texts published during these first years, are concerned with the most pressing issues faced by the society at the triumph of the Revolution: 1) "[reflecting] on the past fight against the dictatorship of Fulgencio Batista and 2) the present and social projects of the Revolution" (Lazo 284) vis-à-vis the deteriorated pre-Revolutionary society.

José Soler Puig published in *Casa de las Américas*, the short story "Mercado libre" (1961) in which he portrays class differences, bourgeois abuse and the complicity of the government during the Machado dictatorship of the 1930s.[6] I mention this short story not only because in it the author creates a picture of Cuban life in the 1930s, but also because the story explores the genesis of the revolutionary fervor that culminates 25 years later. It does so through the character of "he"—a child—who, belonging to the high middle class, repudiates the exploitation of man; analogically the reader understands that "he" is referring to the figures of Fidel Castro (b. 1927) and Ernesto Che Guevara (1928-67). The third-person narrator (the son of the "señora") is very detailed when he communicates descriptively the great differences between social classes represented. In the market of the Plaza Marte where mother and son go shopping in a car with a driver, there are: "women with packages like Tita [the cook that goes shopping for the family] and

---

[6]. Gerardo Machado was constitutionally elected president of Cuba in 1924. In 1928, at the end of his term, he manipulated the other political parties by means of intimidation, coercion and corruption to assure his presidential nomination. In 1928 he was elected to another presidential term and in 1933, he was ousted by a coup d'etat (Pérez, *Cuba: Between Reform and Revolution 248-64).*

women without packages, a bit like momma" (3). The salespeople, on the other hand, have "big faces—black faces, white faces, mulatto faces—without smiles over the shoulders of dirty, torn and patched shirts" (3-4). The characters in the short story are witnesses to an incident during which the police hit one of the vendors repeatedly with a machete; nevertheless, the character "he" is the only one who rejects the incident: "[H]e did not want to keep looking [...] he was cold and trembling. His face burned. He felt like vomiting" (5). In contrast, the "señora" is happy with the incident because she profits from it: "Today we bought three times more than the other day, and with less money [...] The vendors were afraid with the soldiers' beating [...] Maybe next Friday there will be another fight" (8). This story is representative of the period, where the narration is poignant in describing class differences, social injustices and the many marginalities to which a good portion of the population was subjected.

Other short stories that distinguish themselves during this period are "Gracias Torcuatico" (1961) by Nicolás Pérez Delgado (b. 1941) and "El esposo" (1961) by César Leante; in both, the central themes are again the different expressions of violence exercised by the Batista police. However, at the same time, the stories exalt the heroism of the fallen, the majority of which were young people from the different social strata and different regions of the country. It is characteristic of these short stories to have plots and characters that are linear, use colloquial language, no ambiguity and endings that are predicted by the narrator. The latter is interested in making sure that the reader does not get lost in complicated plots, but that he or she may fully grasp the historical realities of the immediate past in comparison with the present day circumstances of the Revolution.

The first short stories of the Revolution are product of a necessity to tell—as the Uruguayan master Horacio Quiroga (1879-1937) would say—to relate and preserve all those episodes of a very near past, painful and lived by the authors. As for the literary form used, this presents, as we have said:

a development that is fundamentally chronological; or a first-person omniscient narrator, or one who is more or less omniscient in third, organizer of the narration, organizer and principal carrier of the information received by the reader; and characters who are sweetly guided by these narrative attitudes. (Redonet, "Para ser lo más breve posible" 8)

THE GOLDEN QUINQUENNIUM: 1966-70

This period is taken over by a new generation of writers, the majority of whom were born around the 1940s, and who recover for Cuban short story writing a position of honor in Spanish American letters. This period was inaugurated by Jesús Díaz (b. 1940) in 1966 when he won the Short Story Prize in the Casa de Américas contest with the book *Los años duros*. Afterwards, three more books appeared with similar themes: *Condenados de condado* (1968), by Norberto Fuentes (b. 1943), and *La Guerra tuvo seis nombre* (1968) and *Los pasos en la hierba* (1970) by Eduardo Heras León (b. 1943).[7] The writers who published during this period are no longer preoccupied with the narration of the aforementioned historical events of the preceding period (except the first three short stories in Díaz's book); the new generation evolves and grows within a man-history dialectic that they have before them, something that does not happen to the writers who publish in the so called Gray Quinquennium (1971-76). Nevertheless, during this golden era, this new generation continues to produce an epic narrative of violence that represents the most recent conflicts in the country reflecting what happened in the Escambray mountain and Playa Girón:
the signs of the new narrative are violence, dissolution of individual characteristics into collectivity, the birth of new values

---

7. Norberto Fuentes' book was awarded the Casa de las Américas Prize in 1968 and Heras's books obtained the David Prize 1968 and a honorific mention in the Casa de las Américas prize in 1970 respectively.

in the consciousness of people involved in the convolutions of the times. (Nogueras 204)

This is a generation whose members reach adulthood witnessing this violence and, after 1959, they realize that to survive and preserve what they have earned, they will have to continue fighting. The voices of their protagonists express the feelings of the nascent revolutionary generation and the historical moment when, like the protagonist of "Mateo," in *La guerra tuvo seis nombres*, they happen to live: "When I realized that I was fourteen years old in a trench, fighting for my country, I thought: I have become a man" (45). On the other hand, this is a group of writers that narrates using narrative techniques inaugurated by the so-called Latin American *literary boom*. In these short stories, the reader is no longer a mere receiver of information, but now becomes an accomplice in the reconstruction of the meaning of the text and the third-person narrator is displaced by narrations that present different points of view and grammatical subjects (first and second persons) thus producing a more "intimate" narrative. Furthermore, the authors accentuate the use of *flashback* and introduce chronotopic juxtapositions, and they also find it of utmost importance to question the consciousness of the characters. It should be mentioned that in the works of these authors[8] we see little influence of magic realism, the fantastic, or the absurd of a Julio Cortázar (1914-84) or a Gabriel García Márquez (b. 1927), but instead, one finds the influence of the Neorealism of Juan Rulfo (1918-86). As in the case of Norberto Fuentes and Eduardo Heras León, some of their short stories come close to a testimonial and/or autobiographical literature—"documentary" as Foster (18) would

---

8. The writer Antonio Benítez Rojo, who in 1967 obtained the Short Story Prize of the Casa de las Américas with his book *Tute de reyes,* is the exception, since he does present a narrative that, although cannot be considered fantastic, does present magic-realism; within the realm of the historical-realism, the author introduces elements that clearly are outside possible reality (Volek 98-99).

call it—that anticipates, but at the same time negates, the strict official exigencies promulgated in 1971 during the Education and Culture Congress. Definitely, it is an innovative narrative that lends itself to different readings according to the ability of each reader and makes use of the "possibilities that the Revolution offers a short story writers that—according to what Cortázar writes in 1962—are infinite. The city, the country, the fight, the work, the different psychological types, the conflicts of ideology and character" (Cortázar 12).

I believe that all of these writers converge in two important points. First, they corroborate the confession of Heras León when he says: "I do not sit down to write just to say something, but rather because I have something to say" (cited in López Sacha "Prólogo" 7). Not simply a word inversion, this statement is the credo that rules this generation of writers who saw and experienced first hand what they describe in their stories. Second, these writers have followed the tradition of the best masters of short story: Poe, Checkov, Maupassant and Quiroga, while incorporating stylistic resources of the most successful Latin American writers: Jorge Luis Borges (1899-1986), Julio Cortázar, Juan Rulfo, Carlos Fuentes (n. 1928), Gabriel García Márquez, Mario Vargas Llosa (b. 1936), thus producing the most powerful and solid Cuban short story not equaled to the present day. On the other hand, these writers who were born around 1940, were motivated by the principal polemics of the first years of the Revolution that turned, as Jesús Díaz confesses to Emilio Bejel in 1982:

> around loyalty to the Revolution. It was a matter of a Revolution, the only one possible, that had accepted to carry things to their ultimate consequence [...] and the second problem in the debate was internal, it developed among those of us who were convinced revolutionaries. (54)

With the aforementioned similarities, there exists a fundamental difference between Díaz's book and those of Heras and Fuentes: in the last two books we find no Manichaeism, but rather a desire to present human beings such as they are, without makeup, without the idealizations present in the socialist realism. Nevertheless, in "No matarás," the last trilogy of *Los años duros,* the author takes as his topic the fights that took place in the mountains of Escambray against the opposition to the regime—a topic that will reach its ultimate expression in the books *Condenados de condado* by Norberto Fuentes and *Los pasos en la hierba* by Eduardo Heras León. In "No matarás," one observes an explicit intention to present the "bandits" in the worst possible light, devoid of any positive characteristic. They are the *rapists*: "That little country girl that I took [...] but since there were three of us, no one knows who got her pregnant" (118); *ruthless assassins*: "you had hanged him [the farmer] from the balsa wood tree with [barbed] wire around his neck and had put a knife [through his wife's neck] so she would not speak" (121-122); *pimps*: "the only thing that I know well, linked to a gringa, one of those well endowed blondes that we see in movies, I put her in business and live from the take" (119). Meanwhile, these bandits idealize at all costs the revolutionary characters that always finish through justice, consideration, valor, and serenity.

I must comment, although briefly, about Heras León's books, who, following the award to *Los pasos en la hierba,* became the object of strong criticism and heated polemics—that will signaled the direction in which the short story, and Cuban literature in general, would follow in the 1970s. Present in the six short stories that comprise the book *La guerra tuvo seis nombres* is the interest on the part of the author to solidify the experiences of two groups of men—the militia (recruits) and their commanders—and the manner in which they interrelated to obtain victory or failure in each situation. For example, in the short story entitled "Piedra," the second in command is forced to take over the position of authority after the death of the Captain during combat in Playa Girón. The ideological conflict is presented when the former is not able to assume leadership "because suddenly he had tried to lead and could not because he had begun to sob" (29-30). Similarly, in the short stories comprising *Los pasos en la hierba,* Heras León presents his characters' human, psychological characteristics in a still stronger manner, thus allowing the observation, through multiple situations, of those who have not understood the new responsibilities that the exercise of power brings, thereby demystifying the idealization—one of the characteristics of socialist realism—emphasized in other stories. This form of narrative, one practically without prejudice, disappeared in literature published in Cuba until the middle of the 1980s—a time when the *Novísimos* began to publish their writings—corroborating what Redonet affirmed in the above cited quote concerning the fact that the Gray Quinquennium lasted until 1982. Within this thematic frame, these short stories are contestatory since they reject—albeit by omission—the a priori defense or exaltation in literature of everything that has to do with the Revolution.

In "El viaje ha comenzado," the last story in *Los pasos en la hierba,* the narrator goes back in time to relate short vignettes containing different situations that remain in his memory during the last few months of his life which support the contestatory position that I propose is found in the collection. One finds this contestatory position in the cases of the revolutionary militiaman "Mario," accused of stealing a pair of boots (126-27); the unhappiness and insurrection in the camp expressed by the narrator: "I think about the men lying on the humid grass, this unhappiness, the idea of fleeing from the camp. I think about Lieutenant Juan Bautista […] ordering to open fire at the first attempt to flee" (129); the intransigency of the Captain and the licensing of the insubordinate militia (131-32); the demystification of the figure of the officer, bringing about a questioning of absolute power on the part of the narrator: "suddenly I discover that they are like us" (132-33); the militiaman narrator that judges his superior, confronts him face to face and, by analogy, provides a criticism of the coercive Cuban system:

> Miguel, who does not speak to us, who does not know how to impose order except through the force of written reports, because that day, alone, under the powerful shadow of the fort's walls, I

shouted to him, 'you are miserable, Miguel! [...] Learn how to be more of a friend and then you will become a man!' (125)

The themes explored by Eduardo Heras León in his short stories cost him his position at the Editorial Council of *El caiman barbudo*, and finally, he was sent to work as a laborer for three years in the factory "Vanguardia Socialista." These actions and others that I will discuss below are the precursors of the Gray Quinquennium in Cuban short story.

THE GRAY QUINQUENNIUM: 1971-76

The critical representation, or better, the adjustment of historical reality, absent in the short stories included in *Los años duros* by Jesús Díaz,[9] but found in Norberto Fuentes and Heras León's books, is not a product of a consciously ideological critical effort against the Cuban government as was the case in 1968 with the books of Herberto Padilla (b. 1932), *Fuera de juego,* and Antón Arrufat (b. 1935), *Siete contra Tebas*.[10] Nevertheless, the reactions against Heras León—and against all cultural productions that were considered "contrary to the Revolution" were many since Cuba had entered a cultural period comparable only to the worst soviet

---

9. The tentative position toward the Revolution in the writings of Jesús Díaz will change a couple of years later when he publishes in *Casa de las Américas* a short story entitled, "Asma" that deals with the death of an asthmatic young man who during military maneuvers, has an asthma attack but is forced to crawl through a field. When he raises his head to catch his breath, a bullet crosses his cranium. Later, in 1973, Díaz will have strong opposition when trying to publish *Las iniciales de la tierra* (initially titled Biografía política). He was able to publish it in 1987.

10. During this year, both writers obtained the literary prizes awarded by the Cuban Union of Writers and Artists (UNEAC) in poetry and theater respectively. These prizes were awarded under protest from the executive committee of the UNEAC for considering both books "ideologically contrary to the Revolution" (Comité Director de la UNEAC 7).

Stalinism, when aesthetics became confused with politics.[11] A clear example of this bridging are the norms for the short story contest "XVI Aniverario 26 de Julio" from the year 1970, won by Manuel Cofiño (b. 1936) with the book *Tiempo de cambio,* which was prefaced with the following statement:

> It must be pointed out also that in this contest we have taken into account the political content as well as the artistic quality of each work as we awarded the prizes; aspects that constitute the fundamental norms of our criteria and of our aspirations. (Dirección Política 8)

One year later, in the First National Congress on Education and Culture held in Havana, the previous criteria became stronger in the resolutions taken to assure the strictly political character of the criteria through an open censorship ideology that has no aesthetic foundation whatsoever:

> it is important to revise the norms of the literary contests [...] and the criteria according to which prizes are awarded [...] We must establish a rigorous system of invitation of foreign writers and intellectuals to avoid the presence of persons whose work and ideology are against the interests of the Revolution. ("Declaración del Primer Congreso" 7)

From this moment on, the political-ideological directive of the Revolution would establish the framework and the direction that the different cultural institutions, including writers, should follow.

The results of the new Cuban cultural policy were predictable. Some writers left then or years later for an uncertain life in exile: Edmundo Desnoes (b. 1930), Antonio Benítez Rojo (b. 1931). Others like Heras León, Heberto Padilla, Belkis Cuzá Male,

---

11. Eduardo Heras León did not publish again until 1977; this time the text was *Acero,* a collection of short stories that inaugurates the writing about the life and work in Cuba's factories.

Reinaldo Arenas (1943-90), were silenced when they were unable to publish or work in any cultural institutions. Furthermore, there was a third group that included Norberto Fuentes, Virgilio Piñera, José Lezama Lima, that did not publish anything until several years later when the founding of the Ministry of Culture in 1976 launched an effort to recover writers who had been marginalized up to that point—but by that time some of them were already dead.

The question that comes to mind is, what short stories were published in Cuba during this period? Contemporary Cuban critics like Francisco López Sacha, Salvador Redonet, Arturo Arango and Leonardo Padura Fuentes agree that the work "young" new writers, such as Armando Nieves Portuondo, Enrique Cirules, Reynaldo Hernández, Imeldo Alvarez García—names that never had any transcendence in Cuban letters—published during this time is of very little aesthetic value, since they fundamentally followed the coordinates traced by the complacent and insipid socialist realism. Therefore: "Reality became free of conflict as did literature, and a rhetoric was proliferated that drew clear distinctions between good and evil, an enlightened present and an infamous past, thereby strangling [Cuban] narrative for many years" (Padura 39). A perusal of the journal *Casa de las Américas* confirms these observations. Between the years of 1972 and 1974, this journal only published seven short stories written by Cubans and not a single one takes daily life into consideration or confronts the new conflicts that the Revolution was facing during these years. They simply recounted the subjects patented during the 1960s but were artistically inferior to the narratives of the Golden Quinquennium.

As Eduardo Heras León explains in a recent interview, the decline in the aesthetic value in narrative is not exclusive to this genre:

> Also in poetry, instead of a pure poetry, a combative poetry, it degenerated into a bucolic poetry. Here we used to call it a poetry "tojosita," because the *tojosa* is a beautiful bird that lives in the country side of Cuba, a bucolic setting. There were very

few important books in this period, in general the period was very gray. (Clark)[12]

THE NEW LITERARY PROCESS

From 1975 on, a new generation of young writers began to forge its way into Cuban letters. The first to appear were Rafael Soler (1945-75), Mirta Yáñez and Rosa Ileana Boudet, who told stories about contemporary life from the point of view of children and, in later stories, of adolescents. Nevertheless, it is not until the writers of the so-called "1980s promotion" or the "*penúltima generación*" (next to the last promotion)—as Arturo Arango, one of its members argues—that one can observe a recovery of the aesthetic successes reached during the Golden Quinquennium and by the narratives of the so-called Latin American *post-boom*. The first to distinguish themselves were Miguel Mejides (b. 1950), Senel Paz (b. 1950), Franciso López Sacha (b. 1950), Abel Prieto (b. 1950), Reinaldo Montero (b. 1952), Aida Bahr, Guillermo Vidal (b. 1952), Marilyn Bobes (b. 1955), and Aída Bahr (b. 1958), young people born mostly in the early and mid 1950s. This group stands out by the honesty with which it attacks historical reality: "they question it from an essentially ethical perspective committed only to the aesthetic responsibility of the artist, who himself was committed to his reality" (Padura 39). The first narratives, as in the case of Miguel Mejides, *Tiempo de hombres* (1978) and Senel Paz, *El niño aquel* (1979), deal with themes that go beyond the borders of revolutionary experience or political ideology: death, the life of children, fear, rural environment; in other words, they are subjects of literary and temporal transcendence.

Senel Paz was in the literary vanguard of his generation during these years: "to speak of Senel Paz's writing—Iraida López points out—is to refer to the most promising Cuban narrative, for the

---

12. For the complete interview, see Clark, Stephen. "Conversación con Eduardo Heras León." *La insignia* (2000).

authenticity and freshness with which the author approaches seriously the literary enterprise; [he is] a born writer" (42). In 1979, Paz's *El niño aquel*, won the "David" Short Story Prize given annually to promising young writers of Cuban literature. These initial stories were followed by the publication of his first novel, *Un rey en el jardín* (1983), and five short stories that appeared in different literary journals: "Vacaciones," "Alicia Alonso baila en mi cabeza," "Rodolfo" (whose title he changed later to "Una historia complicada"), "No le digas que la quieres" and, finally, *El lobo, el bosque y el hombre nuevo,* winner of the Juan Rulfo Award in 1990 and published in book form in Mexico and Cuba.

The short stories collected in *El niño aquel* (ENA) are presented from the gaze[13] of a child protagonist who narrates them. Among the seven short stories there is also an affinity of topics and concurrent signs whether they be in space (austerity inside the Republic before the Revolution) or in the narrative time, where one finds a montage of the present and the past (Paz includes occasionally abrupt movements in grammatical time within the narrative: past-present-future-past but always with events that occur before the Revolution); there is the juxtaposition of present characters (the grandmother, the mother, the sisters) and absent ones (male figures). One also finds in the stories marked contrasts among social classes, and the recurrence of symbolic elements (laces, colors, butterflies, umbrellas, cocoons). The child that acts as narrator-protagonist invites the reader to enter into the psychological subjectivism of infancy, so that the narratee "lives" the child's tensions that in some cases may have some affinities with the reader's own tensions. Without becoming fantastic, the gazer includes in his childish way episodes that "[are] carried through [his] thoughts" ("Bajo el sauce llorón" ENA 10). Also possible in

---

13. A view that according to Geral Genette, possesses: "a degree of abstractness which avoids the specifically visual connotation of 'point of view'" (Rimmon-Kenan 71).

his world are conversations, "dialogues," with animals, plants and flowers:

> "Hey! Where is he going all spruced up? Does he think that he is Mundito Gutiérrez?" said the hens when they saw me leaving. But I did not pay attention to them and told the carnations to open [...] and I told the butterflies to stand guard and fly as soon as Papa arrived, and I told the cats that each should hunt a mouse. (ENA 13)

I have alluded to the protagonist role in the narration of the events, but I must clarify that in many cases, besides observing and narrating the perceived events, the child is a "participant witness" (Ibargoyen 67) and is susceptible to the surrounding events which, at times, causes him despair without comprehending them. For example, in the short story cited before, the return of the child's father, whom he does not know, is announced. Paz creates in the narration an environment of rising excitement in the protagonist before the announced arrival. On different occasions and in different ways, the child imagines how the father will react on seeing him, but always noticing his "manhood" is of foremost importance: "'Who is this man who is so serious and respectful who has stopped there?', Papa will ask. 'This is your son!' grandmother will answer. 'Don't tell me: how big and how handsome! Run here, son, I want to greet you and give you the gifts that I brought you.'" The tension mentioned above achieves a literary climax only to fall abruptly and to transmit to the reader the suppressive disillusionment that results from the evident rejection: "'jumping eyes like his mother's family', say [the father], closing the circle of **his** family, and they all walk toward the house" (20). The childhood vulnerability of the characters also becomes clear in the face of the grandfather's death ("Mama speaks without flowers on her hair"), the temporal absence of the mother and the sisters, and on another level, this vulnerability surpasses the barriers of the familial plane to enter the issue of differences in classes ("Miedo al mar" and "Almuerzo") as perceived from the perspective of the son of the servant.

Paz moves away from narrating the childhood world when he publishes the short-story, "No le digas que la quieres" and later *El lobo, el bosque y el hombre nuevo;* in this stories he focuses on the particular world the Cuban adolescents. Similarly, the rural space is replaced by urban areas or small towns, while the action takes place during the years following the Revolution.

On the political-ideological level, these short stories have a contestatory agenda that is absent from his earlier writing. According to Gerardo Mosquera, this phenomenon does not appear only in Paz's narrative, but it is a product of the new Cuban art that awakens during the 1980s:

> The first surprising thing about the new Cuban art is that it begins and establishes a critical consciousness that had not been publicly pronounced. This is not done in a judgmental way: the art simply presents problems that people discuss on the streets and that remain quite absent from the discourse of mass [media] distribution, public assemblies, and classrooms. (60)

Senel Paz can corroborate Mosquera's assertion in his last short story, in which one finds underscored issues that were discussed by common citizens but not with government authorities at that time: discrimination, censorship, and a closed society. At the end of the story, Senel Paz goes beyond a simple contestatory allusion. Directly, but ingeniously, he puts words in the mouth of the marginalized—as it is the case with Diego, the gay man who is forced into exile. Senel Paz presents an explicit criticism of the Cuban government and a calling to the youth for a new revolutionary consciousness:

> You will ask me who am I to speak to you this way. But yes, I have moral values; one time I told you that I am a patriot and a Lezamite. The Revolution needs people like you, because the Yankees, no, but gastronomy, bureaucracy, the type of propa-

ganda that you do and arrogance, all can bring this [Cuba] down, and only people like you can help to stop this downfall. (57)

In the story "No le digas que la quieres," the fundamental axis is the treatment of love between adolescents. The protagonist, Pedrito, is a student who recounts the preparations for the first sexual experience with his girlfriend, Vivian, and the effect that this has on his classmates, "Arnaldo told everyone that that night I would sleep with a woman" (107). In an extraordinary way, Paz leads the reader through the corridors of the world of masculine adolescence, sending him or her—as Cortázar would say—to "that fabulous opening from the small to the large, from the individual and what is circumscribed to the very essence of the human condition" (8). The psychological treatment of an erotic-sexual initiation for the protagonist begins with the advice of a more experienced friend: "Arnaldo had explained to me three or four things that you have to do to women" (107), and it ends with the consummation of the sexual act that coincides with the loss of juvenile innocence: "at the last moment, we saw or felt [that two children] taken by the hand were distancing themselves, they walked over us, she with her belt in her hand, had lost her umbrella" (118-19).

By using extremely sensual language and taking advantage of the imagination of the protagonist, the author recreates, in a marvelous way and with highly poetic language, the loss of virginity, achieving, at the same time, a great equilibrium between the "sordid environment of the inn, where the act is consummated, and the emotional, ethic, and erotic contents of the act" (Ibargoyen 68). A synthesis between the "imagined" and the "real" is achieved in such a way that, during a first reading, one has difficulty distinguishing the levels of narration. Along with the central plot of adolescent love, Senel Paz explores the ideological thought of the student population of the Island toward the end of the 1960s, the historical time in which the narration occurs. The major concerns of the students portrayed in this story range from "love," the subsequent sadness after the death of Che Guevara (112-13), the internationalist anxiety (111), militancy, to the Communist Youth Union and the repudiation meetings (110), all themes that the *Novísimos* will revisit in their narratives. Finally, in "No le digas que la quieres," Senel Paz presents the many realities[14] and social responsibilities of each student, and in this process, he assumes a critical attitude about the pressure to become a productive member of society and thus achieving the ideal of the Guevarian New Man; as Arnaldo says to the protagonist at one point: "the world needs you to take better care of it" (111).

Besides implementing a first person narration, Senel Paz frequently uses dialogue and therefore, as Emil Volek theorizes, creates dialogic characters,

> they are not simply jailed in their own teleologies (or theologies) [...] but they react to each others words or even anticipate them; they actively exchange information and they elaborate inside their own teleological semantic systems the information, and as a result, they enrich each other. (*Metaestructuralismo* 109)

Also, as one can appreciate in "No le digas que la quieres," Paz uses the "dialogue of the absent character" (109), who is the reader himself. The narrator takes a friendly position toward the narratee, with whom he pretends to have a close relationship; for example, he addresses him as *compadre*: "hey, this is beautiful, *compadre*, why did I not think of it?" (113). On other occasions, he questions the reader, asking for an answer to his question: "don't you talk about these things with your girlfriend?". Using this narrative technique, the author succeeds in asking for a more active partici-

---

14. Emil Volek states: "Since even the 'reality' of a simple object is infinite, even the most realist model is always a cut and patch: it interprets, chooses, classifies aspects and, in fact, creates a simulacrum of reality as one believes that it exists; it is a model of simulacrum" (*Metaestructuralismo* 9). Also, Cortázar's opinion is valid: "a story in the final analysis, moves from this level of the man where life and written expression of this life engage in a fraternal battle" (5).

pation by the narratee, who in turn pays more attention to what is being read. Benítez Rojo's theory about the double seduction that occurs in literature supports this observation: "In each reading, the reader seduces the text, transforming it, making it his own; in each reading the text seduces the reader, transforming him, making him its own" (XXX).

As I made clear at the beginning of this chapter, since 1959, the Cuban short story has been subjected to the movement of a pendulum that obeyed a politico-ideological maxim and was not judged by its aesthetic value. A chronological analysis of this pendulum allows one to see the close relationship that the short story has had with governmental ideology as well as with the history-man dialectic, and how these factors have had influence on thematic choices and the stylistic resources used for their development.

I conclude with a note of optimism, knowing that the short story writers that began to publish after 1980—also called the "*narradores de la búsqueda*" (writers of the search)—have a preoccupation with finding new styles and themes that will question a not so distant past and a very complex present. The themes broached are varied, from everyday occurrences like conflicts between couples to more extraordinary events like the drama of exile, as well as a series of other themes and critical explorations not broached earlier: homoeroticism, corruption, bureaucracy, lack of freedom, rock music, individualism, prostitution, and internationalism. These themes, together with a stylistic development of high quality, promise that the new generations of Cuban writers will surpass the successes reached during the Golden Quinquennium. Only time will affirm or negate my conjecture.

CHAPTER 3

THE CUBAN SHORT STORY OF THE *NOVÍSIMOS*

INTRODUCTION

Cuban short story writing reached a key point in its evolution with the literary production of the young writers born between 1959 and 1972, called the *Novísimos* by Cuban critic, Salvador Redonet. These writers set aside the traditional themes and forms of literature about the Cuban social dialectic—internationalism, the fight against dissidents in Escambray, espionage, anti-imperialism, workers' sacrifice—in favor of other topics of more contemporary transcendence which allow for a degree of literary experimentation that abandons linear practices and demands from the reader a greater reflection about the text from a social and formal standpoint. In the essay "Crónica de antaño," Cuban writer and critic, Francisco López Sacha, recognizes that this generation is comprised of iconoclast, irreverent writers not bound by narrative tradition; as López Sacha argues, the present short story no longer assumes:

> Roundness, perfection, impact, but is instead an amalgamation in style, with an absence of dramatic crisis or conclusion, and comprised of complex thematic variations devoid of a center and a treatment of history as if it were of no importance. (47)

I make the previous statements understanding that rigorous parameters for defining this new literary promotion still need to be established due to its short existence, and, even more importantly, one must acknowledge that, even at the present day, this group has not reached its highest level of achievement. The absence of available texts hinders a more comprehensive analysis of the *Novísimos*. It is true that the writers have been at work for more than fifteen years, but a large portion of their texts have never been published or were only produced in limited quantities. Until 1993, there were only two anthologies, of limited circulation, that are completely or primarily dedicated to the *Novísimos*. The first one was compiled by the narrator and screen writer Senel Paz (b. 1950) *Los muchachos se divierten* (1989) and the second one from 1993, was edited by the literary critic Salvador Redonet and entitled *Los últimos serán los primeros*. One must take into account that these young "unknown" writers have found themselves compared to the literary values set by such writers as Miguel Barnet, Lisandro Otero, Marilyn Bobes, Senel Paz, and Leonardo Padura Fuentes, and must compete with these writers for inclusion in the literary journals and anthologies that are still published in Cuba.[1]

In some Cuban cultural circles with clear official affiliation the innovative literary force that charges the *Novísimos* has been interpreted as irreverent or disillusioning. Such is the opinion of the narrator, poet an ethnologist Miguel Barnet,[2] who in an

---

1. The widespread paper shortage has severely limited the production of what was once a Mecca for publications in Latin America. It must be said that from 1997 to the present different cultural organizations world wide are absorbing the printing cost of many of the journals and books, such *La gaceta de Cuba, Revolución y cultura, Nuevos narradores cubanos,* and many others.

2. Miguel Barnet earned the National Prize in Literature in 1995. Among his better known works are: *Biografía de un cimarrón (*1966), *La canción de Rachel* (1969), *Gallego* (1981)—all testimonial novels—as well as the poetry collections, *La piedra fina y el pavorreal* (1963) and *Orikis y otros poemas* (1980). In 1989, he published his most recent

interview surprised me with his opinion that there are not "any successes in the new Cuban narrative [...] Nothing new has come about [...] Lies are not information nor are they innovation." However, from my intensive readings, I have come to a diametrically opposed conclusion: the new Cuban short story writer is interested in and brings about existential reflection about his contemporary setting, and he reconceptualizes his social cosmos. Loneliness, anguish, lack of direction or a future are all recurring elements incorporated into situations that reflect present-day Cuban reality: the warlike internationalization, foreign tourism, the marginalized worlds of prostitution, rock music, drugs, and homosexuality. As one can see, the vestiges of socialist realism, present in literature decades before, are absent in these writers.

It would be unjust to limit the analysis of short story innovation, since the *Novísimo's* discourse is a confluence of thematic and formal innovation. That is, the *Novísimos* posit strictly related themes with their personal experiences and do so through new narrative strategies: the formulation of questions, dialogues with the reader, the apparent fracture of time and space, the creation of absurd texts that border on the incoherent; as López Sacha (b. 1950) says, "the stories no longer appear to be stories in the traditional sense; they are another kind of story." An example is the short story, "Escrituras" by Rolando Sánchez Mejías (1959) that "[may] be read as a poem and also as an essay. The short story [progresses] without a plot, in abrupt digressions, and one of them [states] the plot" (López Sacha 49).

The texts that I analyze in this chapter were chosen according to two fundamental criteria. The one that most determined my choices was the availability of the published texts. To obtained them, I researched several Cuban journals: *Casa de las Américas, Unión, La gaceta de Cuba, Revolución y cultura, Cúpula,* and *El Caimán barbudo,* but it was the journal, *Letras cubanas* from number 9 on (1988 until it stopped being published in 1995), that

---

novel, *Oficio de angel.*

has yielded the greatest number of texts, since it is the one engaged in the greatest dissemination of the *Novísimos* writing. My second source is Redonet's anthology, mentioned earlier. The second criterion has more to do with content than form. Since my underlying purpose is the analysis of contestatory elements in Cuban literary production, I am more interested in analyzing those texts that provide a (re)vision of history than those in which the primary interest is formal innovation.

In terms of critical analysis, very little has been written about these stories. In the bibliography, I list a few texts that closely analyze the writing of the *Novísimos*. One of the first critical pieces is the one that serves as an introduction to *Letras cubanas* number 9, written by Arturo Arango and entitled, "Los violentos y los exquisitos" (1988). In the last few years, Francisco López Sacha, Leonardo Padura and Salvador Redonet—leading the way into a new and quite unknown territory—have published other critical accounts of these short stories.

ANTECEDENTS

In an roundtable discussion conducted in June 1994 (see appendix), the writer and critic Francisco López Sacha told me that the last generation of writers is the first one that has not had to live through the traumatizing indoctrination of political dogmatism that circumscribed previous generations of writers. The disturbing experiences that earlier generations of writers had, such as, the meetings with Fidel Castro at the José Martí National Library in 1961, the Education and Culture Congress in 1971 or the traumatic happenings surrounding the Padilla case in 1971 (all episodes which had repercussions within Cuban culture in general during the black decade) are remote events, not witnessed by the latest generation. Therefore, Arturo Arango, who also belongs to the penultimate generation—the "Generación Tardía" (Late Generation), as he has called it—agrees with López Sacha when he states that:

[this generation] was formed in the 1970s, during the Gray
Quinquennium, a time when everything that we are suffering
now was taking root. Consequently, we were brought up within
dogmatism, within sectarianism, bidings which we have had to
break from the inside. That is, we were born with self-censorship
genes. (quoted in Henríquez 19)

Nevertheless, one cannot ignore the fact that the *Novísimos* were "born" under the umbrella of a controversial historical time, the 1980s. The decade began with the massive Mariel exodus that saw more than one hundred thousand Cuban citizens flee to the Southern coast of the United States, event only comparable with the first wave of exiles that left Cuba toward the end of 1959 and beginning of 1960s. Within the national realm, the decade culminated with the judicial processes and subsequent killings of the General and national hero, Arnaldo Ochoa Sánchez, Colonel Antonio de la Guardia, as well as two of their underlings, when they were accused of conspiracy and drug trafficking, and thus treason. One also cannot ignore that, at an international level, the break down of the Soviet Union and the European socialist camp in general greatly affected the social and economic Cuban situations. During this short time period, there were other events that impacted the lives of all Cubans, such as an increase in the already terrible shortages of all kinds of personal articles, including food, electricity, gasoline and the closing down of the popular parallel markets. Furthermore, critical was the end of internationalist military expeditions as well as the Cuban participation in wars in Angola and Ethiopia, the rebirth of "social evils" such as prostitution, drugs and currency traffic. Also problematic was the continuous influx of exiles returning to the Island as part of a plan of family visits that brought about the capitalist phenomenon of market consumption, unknown by all of those who were raised under the umbrella of state socialism that was established at the beginning of the revolutionary period. As one might expect, the *Novísimos* found themselves in the epicenter of these events, not only as citizens, but as artists who devote themselves to the difficult task of analyzing and writing about a constantly changing reality.

It is important to note that the *Novísimos,* while covering new themes, are not in any way a generation of writers without a historical foundation within Cuban literature. It would be incongruous to assume as much. Much the same as the earlier generation—those born around 1950—the *Novísimos* deal with the theme of adolescence, a world that is nearer to their own personal experience. Nevertheless, as shown in the previous chapter, the treatment of the individual adolescent (*la cuentística del deslumbramiento* [the writing of awe]: 1974-79) that begins with the stories of Rafael Soler (1945-75) and is more fully developed by Senel Paz (b. 1950), Francico López Sacha (b. 1950), Leonardo Padura Fuentes (b. 1955), Arturo Arango (b. 1955) and Marilyn Bobes (b. 1955), is transformed by the latest generation through a resistance to formalisms, Manichaeism, outlining and simplifications that before had always been present, to a greater or lesser extent, within Cuban literature of the Revolution.[3] Redonet, in the introduction to the anthology *Los últimos serán los primeros* (1993), agrees with my perception that:

> Thus in the ideo-aesthetic conception of the *Novísimos* there exists a demystifying attitude and a profaning of false values and there is an assumption of authorial perspectives that is viscerally conflicted, de-automatizing: thinking for themselves, affirming their personalities, and their ethical-aesthetic ideals. (22)

It is because of this autonomy, that in the stories that these young people write, the characters are "different"—dissident and mar-

---

3. The writing of the earlier generation mentioned, expressed as much as possible within its historical time, while being unable to approach overtly conflicts that in the 90s they have began publishing in such texts as: *El lobo, el bosque y el hombre nuevo* (1991) by Senel Paz, "Dorado mundo" (1993) by Francisco López Sacha and "Rumba palace" by Miguel Mejides (1994).

ginalized—one could say—to use a more postmodern term. One often finds characters like the *Zombie*, the *Freakie*, the *Punk*, or the *Rocker*, with long hair, irreverent figures who disregard the traditional values, who instead listen to rock, get drunk, and sometimes might consume drugs or who are sexually promiscuous. In other words, this stories present a characterization of youth that is not seen in the idealized literature whose goal is to describe the utopian society of the Cuban "New Man." The new writer tries (and in my opinion succeeds) through his stories to deconstruct—or perhaps—to unmask, the hypocrisy of the official discourse that through the years has attempted to silence certain dimensions of reality. Therefore, in their narrative the *Novísimos*, confront homosexuality, sexual promiscuity, drug addiction, AIDS, the questioning of individual existence, family problems, adultery, corruption, state authority and tourism, as central or collateral themes. I should however clarify that not all these themes are new; an example of this is the continuous thematic preoccupation with the national or international military actions. However, if before the focal point was the collective heroism of the participating characters, what becomes salient now is the personal drama, above all the psychological element. Individuals no longer triumph to ennoble the country, although this may occur; instead, the characters are concerned with complex psychological conditions: fear, loneliness, sexuality, alienation, doubt and other emotions. Internal conflicts or conflicts between a character and those around him replace the conflict of man and history: discourse now centers on the individual.[4] López Sacha says it well in the above-mentioned interview:

> Fundamentally, it is a change in perspective; the conflict is not longer one of history toward the individual, but of the individual

---

4. It should be noted that this focus on the individual was started by the writers of the violence in the Golden Quinquennium (1966-70): Jesús Díaz, Norberto Fuentes, Eduardo Heras León, among others. With the arrival of the Gray Quinquennium, this writing came to an end.

toward history. The "I." First let's observe the individual and then we see what happens to this individual within history.

In chapter IV, where I discuss homoeroticism in Cuban narrative and in Cuban society, I analyze the new writing that moves toward a new theme by deconstructing the veil of propaganda that tries to ignore and oppress the contestatory reality present in society, resulting in a literature that reaches indiscriminately all sectors. Therefore, the present chapter is limited to exploring three narrative levels with their respective socio-political themes that I classify as 1) the representation of reality in the stories of warlike internationalism, 2) the fantastic in the repudiation of foreign tourism, 3) the allegorical techniques for writing about Cuba. I must point out that the reader will notice an uneven distribution of works analyzed within each category: four short stories in the first and one each in the others. When researching the subject matter of the published works during the years covered—not necessarily representative of those works written—one notices the concentration on warlike internationalism. This phenomenon has two logical explanations. First, I have established that the Cuban writer likes to write about his history, about his personal experiences; consequently, because a good number of writers from this generation either participated themselves, or had family or close friends who did so in the missions that Cuba maintained in Africa for more than sixteen years (1976-93), international wars have touched them personally. The result is a great number of narratives that deal with experiences of war, that as we see, place history(ies) of the individual(s) against a possible collective history, as expressed in Francisco López Sacha's last quotation.

SHORT STORIES OF INTERNATIONAL WARS

The representations of combat in the narratives of the Cuban Revolution go back to the years of subversive resistance against Batista in both the Sierra Maestra and in the cities, as we saw in previous chapters. It was expressed earlier that one of the earliest texts with a great impact in those years was a book of short stories written by Guillermo Cabrera Infante, who has been in exile since 1965. *Así en la paz como en la guerra* (1960) contains 15 vignettes and 14 short stories written between 1950-58 in which the author, among other topics, relates various daily confrontations between the rebels and the security forces loyal to the Bastista dictatorship. In the same decade, during the so called Golden Quinquennium (1966-70), the main writers of the time—Eduardo Chinea, Jesús Díaz, Eduardo Heras León, Norberto Fuentes—dedicate their stories to those narratives that recount fights against the bandits of Escambray and the invasion of the Playa Girón, and their protagonists are often members of the revolutionary militia.

I have already said in this chapter that the *Novísimos* try to approximate events that are very much linked to their reality, as were the international expeditions. Thousands of Cuban young people carried out their compulsory military service in Nicaragua or in less known lands, the arid planes of the African continent. Consequently, it is not strange that several of these writers have an intimate knowledge of Cuban military participation in Angola, for example. The necessity of underscoring the relationship of a particular individual with his history becomes apparent in these stories more than in others; therefore, it is characteristic of these narratives to have the narrator exploring in the most profound psychological states of the characters.

The Angolan theme in the *Novísimos* has an immediate antecendent in the story "Según pasan los años" (1989) by Leonardo Padura Fuentes (b. 1955), who belongs to the literary generation of the 1980s. In this short story, one sees for the first time in Cuban narrative, a substitution—albeit slight—of the focus on triumph by a narrative that questions the loss of life or its forced alteration in a young person who is living it to the fullest. The example of Elías, the protagonist, is significant, since when he is "mobilized," he has to leave his university studies and when he returns to Cuba after two years of fighting and having thought "more than once whether he would ever walk again through the streets of Havana" (15), he finds himself in a paradoxical situation. Even though in Africa "he spent his time remembering Cuba and thinking about what [he was going] to do when [he returned]," he now confesses to a loss of direction when his old friend Lucrecia asks:

> And what are you going to do now?
> I don't know, I forgot (12)

The occasion that unites the ex-lovers in Havana one day after Elías's return to Cuba is the sudden death and subsequent wake of Juan Carlos, a friend for twelve years during their high school days. With his discussion of "death," Padura develops the theme of participation in the Cuban war in Angola. In this story, we see exemplified, in an incipient manner, some existential lines at a personal level that the *Novísimos* will develop in their stories: melancholy, fear, longing, pain, and above all, the constant meditation about the possibility of facing death. In one of the conversations with Lucrecia, Elías confesses to her: "Here, it is as if no one dies, as if all of us were to last for two hundred years. There, it was different and one thought: 'will it be me?'" (22). This comment is made during the most dramatic moment of the story, when the protagonist narrates the accidental death of a friend in Angola. One should note that the narrative here is in the first person, creating a more intimate, testimonial effect and transmitting in a more vivid way the fatal encounter with the land mine, an event that could have occurred to any of those belonging to the present platoon: "The best friend that I had in Angola died within a few meters of me. We were taking surrounding the enemy lines and he stepped on a mine. What we recovered were little pieces of a person" (21). I reiterate that this story begins a thematic strand within what could be called the "new" story of violence, that of the individual's constant existential preoccupation before a history, a theme which is being carried out more fully by the writers from the lastest generation.

A fundamental characteristic of these stories about international wars is the rejections and subsequent substitution of the epic-heroic (triumphalist) with the development of the most cruel psychological battles. These wars originate inside the human being himself, who questions his reason for being within a situation that is limited by what is required of him. In this section, I have chosen to analyze four texts: "El día de cartas" (1988) by Roberto Luis Lastre[5] (b. 1958); "La noche del mundo" (1988) by Rolando Sánchez Mejías (b. 1959); "Sueño de un día de verano" (1990) by Angel Santiesteban (b. 1966); and, "Espejo de paciencia: (1995) by Alberto Guerra[6] (b. 1963). Although the dates mentioned are those of the publication of the stories, they do not necessarily represent the year in which they were written. A chronological view shows that the thematic that Padura began in the 1980s continued for several years afterwards by younger writers.

Roberto Luis Lastre's text, "El día de cartas," is very interesting and innovative in ways that differentiate it from the other three mentioned. The struggle (violence) presented is internal, within the character himself, with his memories and with his future. As the title suggests, the narrative focuses on the greatly desired routine of receiving and (re)reading the letters from loved ones while one is abroad serving in a military mission. Thus the author, without making any direct mention of the daily phenomenon of physical death, reveals another kind of death, one of a psychological nature that affects the men who do not receive any letters: "Here everyone came to get fucked [...]. Besides the letters, a weekly film can become life" (97). It is through the lines written by the wife, in this case, that the protagonist—whose name we never know, since he is one and all men at the same time—maintains contact with his

---

5. In spite of the fact that Lastre was born a year before 1959, I have included him in this section and grouped him with the *Novísimos* since his text is one of the first ones to address the theme from this perspective.

6. I should mention that his war story belongs to the book *Aporías de la imagen* that won the Special Prize of *La gaceta de Cuba* during the 475th anniversary of the University of Havana contest.

former world, whose existence he begins to question because of the time that has elapsed. The soldier says that in one letter, his wife describes the house "so that he will not forget and for a moment he may sit in his red armchair, in front of the television, while she drinks a soft drink and crosses her legs on the sofa inciting an assault." Nevertheless, his memory is fragmented from all the months he has been away from home, and relegated to a hostile world; he ask himself if "[T]hese things, armchair, sofa, television, soft-drink, [...] exist in the world?" (97-98). These soldiers are men who have been "mobilized," as Padura's short story explains. They are abused, separated from their friends, loved ones and the environment in which they grew up and lived and are sent to a faraway world in which everything is foreign. Lastre's short story succeeds in communicating to the reader that the existence of the man in Angola is limited to the "framed photographs that [he loves] and [carries] throughout the world to show what [is] his past. It is the mask with which [he unmasks] his identity" (98). The life of the characters are bound to a past of memories that are renewed each time a letter arrives or an old letter is re-read.

One of the most controversial themes in stories about military missions that require prolonged conjugal separation is that of sexual loyalty; Lastre deals with this subject also. The solitary man confesses that he has resolved his "problem" using his imagination through the invocation of the memory of his wife, probably provoked by a couple kissing in the weekly film. Nevertheless, this same "kiss that they give each other is the kiss that he misses" (97), a confession from the protagonist, which communicates the need for physical-psychological closeness that is affecting him. This strong sexual necessity is resolved through masturbation, mentioned on two occasions. In one of them he confesses that when he thinks about his wife "maybe he masturbates. The soldiers masturbate with dirty hands" (97). He uses the plural, making the reader understand that this sexual side, so strong in a human being, is a normal condition and it is no longer a taboo subject to be ignored. On a second occasion, the protagonist admits the diversity of his sexual fantasy that has driven him to satisfy his desire in places associated with the war front: "If she knew that I've jerked off even in the trenches" (98). Once again, Lastre presents what has always existed, human necessity, introspection, many faceted fears, doubt, instead of the heroic triumphant portrayal of war found in previous stories. In a brief instance, the soldier is troubled by doubt when he asks himself: "and she…" (98); he confronts the possibility that his wife may not be satisfied with masturbating as he is and may be going to another man in his absence, thus bringing about an internal conflict in a man who feels that his virility and the patriarchal institution to which he subscribes would be violated by her infidelity.

In the entire short story, there is only one case of traditional warlike violence. Nevertheless, this violence comes as a psychological and not a physical attack. Echoing the title, the first line of the story warns the reader that the events take place during a special day for the soldier: "It is letter day" (96). From this sentence, the afore-mentioned allusions will branch out, but what is most important is the arrival of the foreign mail truck. As I noted in the beginning, the tragedy of the character is primarily internal; in this last instance, the catalyst for this tragedy is the destruction "of the mail truck by a mine," resulting in the loss of the much needed family contact: "The kisses that they sent us. The photographs of the children's birthdays […] The fragments of friends. Infinity. Don't cry" (99). Such psychological tragedy is compared by the protagonist to physical pain that clarifies his feelings for the reader: "A cigarette burn to the pupil …," he stutters, finishing with the phrase that is no longer embued with the hope of the initial line: "It was mail day" (99).

This narrative's protagonist is a man who is bound by laws conceived by others—the international mobilization, in this particular case—and who is consistent with the *Novísimos'* proposal of maintaining individual history as the central concern of the discourse. Also, it is true that Lastre seeks to present man, such as he is, with his faults and successes, leaving aside eloquent passages about heroism present in some of the first short stories about violence from the 1960s. I reiterate that the innovative detail in this short story is the exploration of the possibility of internal violence in two different geographical spaces, Cuba and Menongue, that are united by the experiences of a man, his memories, and the letters that transport him to a past that, for him, seems unreal, non existent. The official story transmitted by the protagonist in this case is that Angola is the heterodiegetic space (as opposed to the utopian, referential one created by his memories and letters from Cuba) that send us to a Dantesque inferno:

> Menongue has the face of an evaporated land and allows each minute to pass like an annoying wait […]. What is nearest is farthest, separated by this passage that is a thorn decorated by a crown of thorns. (96)

A second example, following the chronological order of publication, is the short story "La noche del mundo" (1988) by Rolando Sánchez Mejías. Different from the other narratives, this short story deals with changes in the narrative planes of space and time with such frequency that the reader occasionally feels decentered. Nevertheless, the story follows the praxis of the previous ones by presenting vignettes of a very personal history situated within the broader context of experiences in Angola. Divided into four short segments, the story is always narrated by an omniscient third person narrator and there appear several characters who in one way or another are related to the protagonist: the young lady with whom he has his first erotic experience in secondary school and who he re-encounters after returning from Angola; the political attaché of the regiment; the dwarf woman who is raped by four soldiers; and, finally, the pottery teacher who is a kind of philosopher/bureaucrat and who questions, "What is truth?" (104). This inquiry points to the most contestatory criticism in the short story, by challenging the State's authoritarian role in establishing rigorous parameters-manichaeistic—without permitting the citizen to question or observe a different posture, let along contrary.

As in the previous stories, Sánchez Mejías makes the obligatory mention of the fact that the university studies of the young man are truncated because: "In 1977 he is drafted into Military Service" (100). I reiterate that this is not a capricious reference on the part of the *Novísimos*; rather it is the need to express an event that has affected this generation of young people, either through the writer's personal experience or that of a family member or a close friend. This same factual basis is seen in the constant references to death, that in this case, falls on the character Rivas, the protagonist's roommate who dies when he "steps on a mine in Angola" (101). The difference in the Angolan experience that Sánchez Mejías's story presents is the role of the central protagonist of the narrative; he is neither the vehicle nor carrier of violence, nor is he a traditional soldier who belongs to a platoon that goes to the war front. Rather he is in charge of: "filling the unit's barricades with themes, martial positions extracted from the regulations, phrases from presentations, didactic scenes with flags/soldiers/bright sky/piece of land" (101). That is, the function of the protagonist is of a political nature and he was given this charge by the "Regiment's Politician" (101). This reference provides a clear indication that political propaganda goes beyond geographical barriers and more importantly the author seems to be reacting against the role of politicking and indiscriminate propaganda in his country, this being the primary reason for the intervention in Angola that he is describing.

In contrast to the previous short story that gingerly touches on the Cuban intervention in Angola, "Sueño de un día de verano" (1990), by Angel Santiestaban Pratts, gives a more concise, detailed—testimonial, one could say—account of the personal experiences that go from the most profound physical pain due to weather: "[our] clothes completely wet and our toes began to split like leprosy from fungus" (164); to the most intrinsic fear of death: "The fear, although hidden, always smells like shit" (165). The multiplicity of narrative voices that, as I have said, points toward a more intimate penetration (in the first person), also promotes diversity in the narrated action. For example, there is a passage in which the author presents, in a consecutive manner, three narrative voices; he begins with the second person, then goes to the first, then finally to the third person:

> As *you* get nearer, the bad smell becomes stronger and *you* like it. And without anyone seeing *me*, *I* unlock the AK and dry my finder and the trigger [...]. *They* touch the guinea grass with the guns. *A head* is raised, shaven almost bald: a woman looks at us without blinking. (165, my emphasis).

The use of this narrative technique in Cuban literature of the Revolution necessarily points one to the novels of Reinaldo Arenas (1943-90). Just as Arenas does in his novel, *El mundo alucinante* (1969), Santiesteban Pratts implements what Emil Volek has called a "cha-cha-cha" of voices[7] (191-201) where, following the theoretical position by Genette, the discourse moves from a heterodiegetic to a homodiegetic plane and vice-versa. That is, in the cited example, the narrator at first is not a participant in the action that he is relating (heterodiegetic); nevertheless, in a second instance, the discourse moves to a more subjective level, that of the first person, and the protagonist himself recounts his experience (homodiegetic) only to move into a third person perspective that de-subjectifies the narrative of events. Also, one can see that within the homodiegetic space, the time of the enunciated is the same as that of the enunciation (intradiegetic), thus creating a larger degree of dramatization and suspense about the event being narrated by the protagonist.[8]

---

7. For further discussion, see the excellent analysis by Emil Volek, "La carnavalización y la alegoría en *El mundo alucinante* by Reinaldo Arenas" in his book, *Metaestructuralismo*.

8. The narrative polyphony observed here is inaugurated in Arena's previously mentioned novel. As an example, I will cite only three sentences from two long paragraphs: "And here is the entire band of mayors following you very closely [...] God and the King [...], listen to those voices that are calling me [...] But the priest seems animated by the

The theme of sexuality in the international missions that Lastre first mentions in "Día de cartas," also finds an echo in this short story, but in a more violent version that involves a third person: the "other." During a raid that the protagonist's platoon makes on a village, the soldiers arrive at a house where they find the two daughters of the owner: "They have two pairs of coffee colored breasts [...]. With a short and light cloth they cover their genitals that were thirsty as ours, [and] caused you to expand until you can't take it anymore and press yourself with your fist in a concealed way" (166). Unlike Lastre's story in which the protagonist's aroused from his wife's memory causes him to masturbate, "Sueño de un día de verano" contains the physical description above quoted that hypnotizes the soldiers making them want, in an action reminiscent of Vietnam, "to be able to discharge" (166) on the Angolan women. The violence transmitted by this reading does not culminate in physical action but is limited to the mental/verbal level because of the presence of the lieutenant—"But the chief agitates and fucks everything"—that keeps them from possessing the girls. This interference causes the narrator to declare in the first person, "Leave us a while longer, bastard" (166). It should be of interest that the narrator both speaks to the characters and also participates in their verbal violence. He tells us that the lieutenant is trying to exchange canned food for meat during the moment of sexual tension, to which the narrator comments, "but you don't desire food, nor rum, nor letters" (166). That is, the narrator understands that what the soldiers want is to satisfy the sexual appetite that is consuming them. In this way, Santiesteban exposes the most intimate desires of the men who go to Angola. One could say that he undresses this young people to present their most personal needs, whether these are seen as positive or negative.

I cannot conclude this analysis without mentioning that, as was the case in "Día de cartas," besides death, one of the most anguish-

---

shout of the mayors, and jumping he goes through to the window" (106-07).

ing preoccupations that the protagonist soldier has in this story is the epistolary contact with Cuba: "Truly what consumes us most are letters from the family, from the girlfriend, or from some friend that may still remember us," a comment that the narrator corroborates by saying: "When they spend days away from the camp, they fear that their letters will be thrown away" (163).

Alberto Guerra writes the last story about which I will comment in this section, entitled "Espejo de paciencia" (1995). This is one of the few stories where we see the characters actually engaged in acts of war. The narrative takes place in an African location. The protagonist is "soldier José Antonio Fascenda, known within the troops as *Flecha* [Missile] (43), who is charged with entering enemy territory to shoot down a plane that is suspected of planning the bombing of the Cuban camp that night. The fist part of the story narrates Flecha's march, his arrival and subsequent wait at the place indicated by Colonel Eudigio Benítez. Throughout the narrative there are sporadic mentions of the protagonist's fear, an element not found in the other stories discussed. Nevertheless, he emphasizes his valor and his unequivocal obedience to his superiors. For example, he has been told, "The other is the *flecha*.[9] They cannot have it. Answer with your life, soldier, so that they will not have it" (43); consequently, the soldier is then willing to risk his life to carry out the ordered mission. The emphasis on the dedication and heroism of *Flecha* is not coincidental, nor are these traits political Manicheisms, since in its conclusion, the story takes an unexpected turn that is consistent with the critical vision of the *Novísimos*.

In a kind of dream or daytime trance, José Antonio is transported to Havana of the future—the reader knows that it is at the end of the 1980s or beginning of the 1990s through references—a city where Sergeant Navarrete has been "converted into an expert driver for one of the corporations [with a car with tinted windows;

---

9. In Spanish, "Flecha" is the technical word in military argot to refer to a missile from the bazooka with antiaircraft capacity.

and] Eudigio Benítez no longer is a colonel, but now is the manager of the corporation" (45). This juxtaposition between *Flecha*'s reality and his fantasy reveals a profound disillusionment. Because of Cuba's involvement in this war, *Flecha* sacrifices himself in a faraway African land for the freedom of third world countries and for the triumph of international socialism, believing everything that has been taught to him since he was a child, only to be transported to a vision of an immediate future where ideals do not count and where the country has sold out to foreign companies. Now his Island is the one invaded.

When he awakens from the trance, *Flecha* decides that "if there is any sense to be gathered from enduring this situation, it is the right to create a different history" (45). The soldier sends a clear message that what he has observed about the events in his country is incongruous with the future planned. He therefore decides to treat this vision as a nightmare and to imagine instead a different future: "Delirium usually puts into men's heads serious crossroads, histories projecting life in a most difficult manner" (45). After recreating history in his own way and deciding to wait until the airplane flies by, the narrator concludes with a sentence quoted before that lets the reader know that what has been imagined is the actual reality. The story ends with a fatalist sentence, defrauding for the protagonist. Lamentably, however it is the reality of the present day Cuban people.

The innovation of war is the concatenation of a glorious past with a moribund present. In his exposition, the author underscores the tragedy that the protagonist lives, not on the front lines as one might expect, but in the shameful failure of the ideals that he defended for years within his country as well as abroad. As the narrator says, the protagonist, as well as the Cuban people on the Island during the last thirty years, "Would never have believed the way they were within ten years" (45).

THE ELEMENT OF THE FANTASTIC

With the last generation of writers discussed in this study, one can perceive how the threads between reality and fiction are severed. Objective realism, so prevalent in the previous years, is not always limited to those stories that are still conventional and follow the classical Quirogan short story. "Sur: Latitud 13" (1993) by Angel Santieisteban and "Ultimo tren a Londres" (1993) by Mariano Torrealba are two clear examples. The need to appeal to fantasy, to fabulation, is present not only as a narrative technique, but more importantly, as a way of expressing truths about Cuban daily life that would otherwise be impossible to convey under a political system dominated by censorship(s). Although there are several short stories that have elements that could be considered fantastic in the *Novísimos* ("Miedo" by Amir Valle Ojeda, "Prisionero en el círculo del horizonte" by Jorge Luis Arzola, to mention only two), one of the stories that best exemplifies the use of elements of the fantastic to delineate contemporary truth is "El señor de las tijeras" (1990) by Ulises Rodríguez Febles (b. 1966). In barely a page and a half, the narrator enters the life of a young Cuban who denounces problems that plague his generation and Cuban society in general: foreign tourism, authoritarianism, lack of diversion, coercion, lack of dialogue.

Before analyzing this short-story, it would be prudent to theorize about what the term "fantastic" means in literature. Tzvetan Todorov posits in his book, *Introduction to Fantastic Literature,* that the many definitions of "fantastic" in literature include "mystery," "the unexplained," "the inadmissible" as they are introduced into "real life," or in the "real world," or yet "the inalterable daily legality" (36).[10] Todorov also writes: "The fan-

---

10. The amalgamation of quotes from Todorov come from P. Castex, *Le conte fantastique en France;* Louis Vax, *El arte y la literature fantástica;* and from Roger Caillois, *Aucoeur du fantastique. I* refer the reader to Todorov's text to find the quotes in their entirety.

tastic is the vacillation experienced by a human being that does not know more than merely natural laws, when he faces an apparently supernatural event" (34). That is, this is a world which is ruled by established physical principles that cannot be violated; human beings under no circumstances can become invisible, nor fly, nor inhabit two temporal or spacial planes at the same time. Nevertheless, fantastic literature authorizes or permits the author to break the established order and makes the reader doubt what he is reading,[11] even if and when the text makes him observe the world of the characters as one of real people and makes him discern between a natural explanation or a supernatural explanation of the events.

In a Latin American context, one cannot ignore the observation made by Julio Cortázar, who, in his essay "Del cuento breve y sus alrededores" (1970), emphasizes that all literary production finds essential support in language. It is in the literary text *per se* that the author creates his particular world by using the tools that language affords him to fictionalize. One must always have this concept in mind when considering the short story in general. Even when a story has a large (or small) basis in the experiential reality of the author, it is always a work of fiction and never a loyal reproduction of this reality. According to the Venezuelan critic Armando Navarro, in "Incursiones en lo ficticio-fantástico" (1992): "Pure realism is a cognitive fallacy, since although the reproduction may begin from artifacts that permit the more or less loyal register of events, such artifacts are not exempt from error" (111). Therefore, when the Colombian writer Gabriel García Márquez takes a living historical character like Simón Bolívar as the protagonist in his novel *El general en su laberinto,* it is no longer Bolívar, the "real person" who lived in the nineteenth century, but a fictitious

---

11. According to Todorov, fantastic literature creates doubt in the reader and makes him question the nature of what he is reading. This is distinct from allegory, where the reader knows that what he is reading cannot be taken literally, thus causing no vacillation (42).

character who is manipulated by the author. García Márquez takes advantage of the freedom accorded to him by language to create a fictitious entity that may or may not coincide with the portrayal of the Latin American hero in history books, texts which attempt to reproduce his life as closely as possible. The Bolívar of the Colombian writer, like all literary characters, has a life that is limited to the duration of the text.

In the previously cited essay, Navarro paraphrases the Peruvian writer Mario Vargas Llosa, who considered in his book *La verdad de las mentiras* (1990), those "literary fictions that act as compensatory mechanisms in which a sense of dissatisfaction makes the individual live, at a symbolic level, those experiences that he desires but cannot realize in the labyrinth of daily life" (114). This quote exemplifies the function of Cuban contestatory literature and it is of special interest in the short story, "El señor de las tijeras." I will analyze this story as a reflection of the experience of present day Cuban society lived by its members and therefore, the text is more than a simple imaginary-fantastic referent. The verisimilitude achieved in the fantastic textual space that marks the narrative results from the inclusion of elements that are literally real:

> If the most realistic story has subjective elements of fiction and fantasy, then in the most fantastical works, the opposite is true. The discourse of greatest fantastic intensity is sustained by a rope that in some way places it in contact with the real or with a kind of truth. (Navarro 112)[12]

The string that connects this short story with reality is found in all those elements that are effectively taken from the real Cuban

---

12. In this case, Navarro is basing his statement on a quote from Alfonso Reyes: "Fiction flies, yes: but like the comet, it is attached to a string of resistance: it never leaves the Universe, nor leaves the "I," nor does it go away from its physical natures no matter how much it becomes thin. These three circles represent the cone, the solid environment of the whirlwind" (Navarro 112).

environment. That is, within a fantastic sphere, one finds a discourse organized on precepts that are verifiable within a real location.

A synopsis of the narrative will facilitate an analysis of the short story. The protagonist in the narrative is Pablo, a young Cuban man who finds himself confronted with the dilemma of trying to decide what to do during his summer vacation that will end the boredom that is draining him. His solution is to let his imagination wonder and "paint what would be ideal: a camp of virgin nature" (150). When the scenery has the necessary elements (colorful cabanas, crystalline river, flowers, green grass), Pablo begins to imagine a paradisiacal dive when a voice stops him and tells him: "if you are not a camper you cannot be here" (150). The verbal threat is complimented by an instrument that represents a potential act of physical violence: scissors that have the capacity to immediately destroy "his" fantastic world (made of poster board). Pablo defies his interlocutor by not obeying him blindly; instead the protagonist questions authority with the dare, "Why?". The answer from the man with the scissors is unexpected: "this is a State institution" (150), which in the Cuban case suggests total sovereignty.[13] At the end of the story, before an insistent questioning by Pablo, the authority cuts the poster board and "left only a lot of dead nature (still life) at his feet" (151).

In an existentialist way, to continue the analytical line from the previous section, this story by Rodríguez Febles again presents the problems of loneliness, lack of social communication, the fight between repression and freedom, besides the evasion of human beings. It would be incongruous with my purpose of contestatory analysis to limit myself to existential study, in its strictest sense, since one of the merits of the young author is to incorporate, within

---

13. When he pronounces this sentence, the man with the scissors begins to enumerate everything that belongs to the State: "mountains, the river, the birds, the air, and he began to give a lesson" (150). By implication, everything belongs to the State, even the protagonist.

a discourse already established by other writers, the great present day conflicts brought about by foreign tourism to Cuba, with all its privileges—vis-à-vis the restricted space, practically without any rights or options, that rules the Cubans who live in the Island.

Literature with fantastic elements has solid roots in Cuba. I need only mention writers such as Onelio Jorge Cardoso (b. 1914), ("El hilo y la cuerda," 1974), or Antonio Benítez Rojo (b. 1931) (*Tute de reyes*, 1967) who during the time in which Rodríguez Febles began to write, were already writers with long and well-known artistic pasts. Nevertheless, the use of the fantastic by these writers, while including chronoscopic transgressions such as in the present case, are different from Feble's, who transmits a message. Its purpose—implicit or explicit—is to raise the consciousness of the individual who is subjugated and voiceless before an authoritarianism that frightens him. The end of the story supports this thesis: after the man with the scissors destroys the fantastic world created by Pablo, the latter has nothing more to do but to return to his "dark room where loneliness and heat have their arms open and filled with desire to embrace him" (151). Nevertheless, the short story ends with the same young man, who on a previous occasion had defied the authority that demanded his exit, trying to defy against the authority that demands his blind obedience by "drawing an answer," that is, arguing against the established order (151).

The ending questions the very concept of evasion that, from a fast reading, could be considered the reason why Pablo begins to paint: to escape the heat and boredom that surround him. However, the last sentence of the story suggests an exercise of individual freedom, of being different, of defying the established order. The young man is not conquered, nor does he allow himself to be intimidated by the initial loss he suffers. Instead, he engages in the act of drawing a response, a reaction that is incongruous with the Stalinist thought that surrounds him; it is here that one finds the global message of the story. The text forces the reader to ask himself, "Against what is Pablo painting an answer?". The work presents several possibilities: the lack of freedom, the abuse of authority, the boredom to which he is subjugated, among others. I believe, however, that there is a more pressing reason: foreign tourism, represented in this story by the Frenchman:

> [Who] ties the speed of the waters as if the tourist had so many teeth as a *saurio* and as if Pablo had to run for fear of the teeth that can only be vanquished by courtesy. (151)

The foreigner, incidentally, emphasizes the aggressiveness of the institutionalized norms because he represents the privileges that he has as a foreign visitor, as opposed to the restrictions placed on the Cuban (the painter) by his government. The image presented by the Frenchman is of particular importance in present day Cuba; he is compared to the *saurio*, an aggressive reptile, backed up by the authority of the man with the scissors. Through this comparison, one understand the relationship between the foreigner and the Cuban government and sees how the tourist possesses prerogatives of pleasure that his national counterpart does not.

The influx of foreign tourism in revolutionary Cuba has not only caused the massive proliferation of a series of social problems that were thought to be extinguished from the Island: prostitution, social inequalities, black market, drug use and trafficking, racial and economic discrimination, but it is also in direct opposition to the doctrine of "Cuba for Cubans" that was preached during the first two decades of the Revolution. An example of this doctrine can be found in the following excerpt from a speech by Fidel Castro in the 1960s:

> Tourists here, to the roulette?
> Tourists here, to the whore houses?
> Tourists, to corrupt? No!

No earning, no economic good can compensate for the moral implications that tourism [...] meant for this country. (Díaz Méndez 10)[14]

It is paradoxical to contrast such unequivocal words with the hundreds of tourist announcements that have been publicized in the last few years in Latin America and by means of social communication in Argentina, Venezuela, Mexico, Italy, France, Canada, Brazil, promoting the exuberant attributes of the "Caribbean pearl." Even more ironic is to find the commercialization of the Island in its own state newspaper *Granma*, through its international edition distributed abroad and in the hotels where foreign tourists stay (tourism advertisement never appear in the editions that go to Cubans, who have no such options). One example that supports my argument is an advertisement that appeared in an international edition of *Granma* in 1992. In this case, the type of trip described is what has come to be known as "ecotourism," announcing that visitors will be able to enjoy:

> Migrating Ducks, Doves, *Yaguasines, Becasines,* Quail and other species in a tropical climate, a clean environment and an important national sanctuary [...] with all the comfort of three and four star **tourist** hotels.(emphasis is mine)

Besides excursions to the beaches, there are artistic and cultural activities. The ad cited textually not only contradicts

---

14. As indicated, the quote was taken from an article published in *El caimán barbudo* in 1972 (its author does not give any bibliographical information to indicate its source), referring explicitly to tourism from the United States before 1959. Nevertheless, this country was not the only one that inundated and contributed to the social "problems" pointed out by Castro. It is important to clarify that, presently, tourism from the United States is welcome in Cuba; on the contrary, it is the American government that prohibits the spending of U.S. dollars by its citizens in the Caribbean island.

Castro's words, but also serves as a segue to the short story that I am analyzing. Rodríguez Febles raises his authorial voice in protest against the exclusivist tourism being sold to foreigners, making the Cuban a second-class citizen; he also questions the voice of authority, as I said before. The ad in question, as well as the short story, explicitly states that anyone who is not a tourist is excluded from this vacationing areas.[15]

The planes of the real and the fantastic are united through different elements from the first that are inserted into the second. One of these elements, situated within the real location (Cuba), is the antagonist, the man with the scissors. Cohabiting the utopian space that Pablo has drawn, this character assumes a canonical discourse that is very aggressive: "If you are not a camper, you cannot stay here […]. Aren't you listening, young man? It is about you […] this is a state institution" (150). By cutting the poster board with the scissors, this antagonist breaks the barrier between the real and the fantastic, unifying the two planes of the story. It is this destabilization of the planes that makes the narrative conflictive. What before was a problem of man and the space surrounding him becomes a conflict of man and man, or more specifically, man and the authoritarian exercise of power.

THE USE OF ALLEGORY

If one accepts the definition of "allegory" as "a narrative or an image that has two distinct meanings, one of which is partially concealed by the visible meaning" (Childers 8), then I would argue

---

15. Note that the mention of the sign "tourist" is understood to be a reference to a foreigner and not to a Cuban resident, who, as it has been mentioned, does not have to option of being a tourist. Note that this tourist can be a Cuban "from the community" who is residing abroad, and since he has dollars, he can buy the tourist packages and enjoy everything that is prohibited to the people who remained on the Island to forge a better future.

that the story "Macaos"[16] (1990) by Enrique Carreño (b. 1963) is an allegorical example of the present day Cuban situation, given the contemporary historical situation and the preoccupation of the *Novísimos* in relating their world, the only world most of them know—it could be argued. In proposing an allegorical interpretation of the story, instead of a symbolic one, I can be accused of a dogmatic posture; nevertheless, my analysis is founded on the continuity of the contestatory trajectory produced by the writers of this generation. To differentiate between symbol and allegory, and to explain my preference for the latter, I depend upon the theories of Paul de Man when he argues that:

> The appeal of the infinity of a totality constitutes the main attraction of the symbol as opposed to allegory, a sign that refers to one specific meaning and thus exhausts its suggestive potentialities once it has been deciphered.(188)

Taking into account the sociohistorical present day Cubans, I believe that "Macaos" presents, in it entirety, a single possible interpretation; therefore, I argue that the story is an allegory such as de Man defines it.

All the analyzed texts in this chapter reflect social conflicts; "Macaos," even when doing so on an allegorical discursive level, is no exception. The first thing that catches the reader's attention is the title "Macaos," which provides the first key to the content of the story. The incorporation of the sign *caos,* (in English chaos), defined in the *Diccionario de la Real Academia Española* as "an amorphous and indefinite state that is supposed to have been before the constitution of the cosmos" (396), exteriorizes from the beginning the problem of the world represented in the story. It is a world without order—aggressive, deformed, violent and repressive—that includes the grotesque Kafkian metaphor of the beetle, representing the individuals who inhabit the place. There is

---

16. I do not cite page numbers for the citations from this story, since it is only one page in length.

no physical description of the space inhabited by these beings. The narrator limits himself to explaining that it is a "little hell," "narrow space," "prison," and "recipient" that contains the beings in a "lower part" since they are all trying to get "to the top."

The words "below" and "above" are opposed not only through the contrary spatial positions, but through their connotations. The first implies the heterotopic (oppressive) space where all are submissive, and the second is the utopian one, the one of physical freedom that all want to reach: "To arrive above, to the top, was the greatest interest, the only way of escaping this little hell." This sentence begins the story. One can assume that the current space inhabited by the characters is oppressive and hostile, and they want to escape it; this desire provokes a violent fight among them: "The most aggressive ones end by making for themselves, above those below them, a place where they can enjoy themselves for a short time, until others, even more savage, take it away from them." One of these more savage individuals, to whom I attribute the role of protagonist, takes advantage of a breach and arrives at the "top of a newly organized pyramid" and "frees himself from what made him similar, from this red spiral." When the individual is already at the point of reaching the space that can be called utopian, "something that looks like a finger [,] shoves him against the opposite wall and makes him fall" near the narrator, "devoid of any salvation." Here one sees repeated the recurrent theme of the negation of the individual that is also seen in "El señor de las tijeras;" the character is oppressed by an exterior political order that dictates his life and either rewards or punishes him.

Taking into account the socio-political and historical contexts in which Carreño lives and writes, and making use of the position of a contestatory reader, I argue that the allegorical space represented in this story is none other than the author's country of origin. Different from "El señor de las tijeras," a work that provides ample references that points to Cuba as the only possible setting, "Macaos" is very ambiguous, and I am conscious of this. Nevertheless, the figures and places that Carreño includes in the story sends the reader metonymically into the real Cuban space.

One asks, for example, why Carreño uses the the figure of an cylinder with tall walls, a symbol of containment and isolation from which one cannot escape. This figure that can be equated with the Island, physically isolated by the waters that surround it and where, no matter how much its inhabitants try, they cannot leave it. Furthermore, the beings that inhabit this world must be comforted by being uniform, without any individual expression possible. The wish of the inhabitants is to reach the utopian space outside the walls that oppress them. However, besides the physical difficulties presented in this space, there is "a finger," a figure that represents authoritarian force that confines them to the assigned heterotopic space. All these connections force me to consider "Macaos" as an allegorical image of present day Cuba.

BRIEF CONCLUSIONS

In the first interview that I had with the poet and editor Juan Nicolás Padrón, he affirmed with patriotic fervor that Cuba is "a village of musicians and poets" "No—he then corrected himself—of poets and musicians" (94), giving a place of honor to Heredia, Martí, Guillén. Adding this statement to the bias commentary of Miguel Barnet cited at the beginning of this chapter (when he refers to the "decadence" of the new Cuban narrative), one could conclude that after Lezama Lima, Lisandro Otero, Miguel Barnet and Jesús Díaz, there has not been any other Cuban writer of relevance. Nevertheless, after analyzing the narratives written by the *Novísimos*—coupled with the later production of the previous generation, including López Sacha, Padura Fuentes, and Arturo Arango, just to name a few—I have to disagree. This last generation of writers specifically, aside from renovating the story telling form, has had the preoccupation of presenting the history(ies) that they live day by day. As one can see by this analysis, besides formal innovation with the use of allegories, parables, the fantastic, the *Novísimo* writer inaugurates the change of perspective that authorizes the characters to present themselves as individuals before a history that surrounds them.

Chapter 4

The Dialectics of Homoeroticism in Cuban Narrative

> Power always seeks an antagonism with some stratum of society. The homosexual is a person who questions the context in which he lives. (Guillermo Cabrera Infante)

> How oppressed people and minorities are treated is a meassure of a society. (Marvin Leinier)

> Apparently, a good Marxist, besides knowing Das Kapital, must demonstrate an impeccable endocrine system. The Party owns his body and soul. The body also includes his genitals and his excretory orifice. (Carlos Montaner)

Revolutionary Conscience

The arrival of what in retrospect can designated as the ideological Cuban revolutionary process is much more than a mere political reorganization from a rightist government to a leftist one; from a politico-economic dependence upon U.S. capitalism to a dependence upon Marxist-Leninist socialism, dominated by the Soviet Union; from a community based on strong family ties to the catastrophic separation caused by the exile of thousands of citizens. Fundamentally, for each individual who decided to stay, or who had no other option but to stay on the Island and, consequently, for all those who were born in the following years, January 1, 1959 marks the beginning of a new identity. I am not referring here to the Cuban nation as a totalizing entity, but rather to the concept of *identity* on an individual and personal level, where each citizen must accept diverse roles but always under the official rubric of "revolutionary," a term which takes on different shades and nuances with the passing of time in accordance with the specific historical period to which it is applied. The social parameters that the State establishes, oftentimes by enacting laws and legal codes, indicate that the Cuban citizen cannot assume his or her own *conscience,* as the Hebrew theorist Tzvi Medin would say. The ideological apparatus that ruled over the Cuban people after 1959 had already begun to take shape with the guerrilla wars in the Sierra Maestra. As is well known, in those initial years of insurgence, formal indoctrination tactics, particularly of the Marxist-Leninist type, did not exist. However, a practical dialectic did; agrarian reform for the campesino, improvement of the quality of life, literacy, and public health programs were all part of the possibility of achieving real change that, for the first time, would benefit the marginalized economic classes.

Even after Fidel Castro took power, there existed no rigorous government plan nor established ideology in Cuba, but rather the notion that the path would be established "en plena marcha" [along the way]. It is for this reason that in 1961, after only two years and four months of revolutionary power, and without consultation with the people or any previous historical precedence, the construction of a new socialist identity was hastily decided: that is, "the construction of what does not exist, or that still does not predominantly exist in civil society" (Fleites-Lear y Patterson 55). With good reason, Fleites-Lear and Patterson ask themselves:

> How can historical reality so radically change by force?, how can one go to bed convinced of the fact that he has defended a

democratic revolution to wake up the next day having defended
a communist one that he is not even familiar with? (55)

To bring the previous observations to bear on the specific theme of revolutionary conscience and identity with which I am concerned, one could ask how it is possible suddenly, the people, by means of unilateral mandate, must conform to the adoption of a new conscience and a new identity, both in a communal and individual sense. This mandate is accompanied by a system of state entities that were put into operation to mold the identity of and to control the Cuban citizens. The task that the Revolution proposes is monumental; in effect it aims to eliminate and replace pre-revolutionary "cancers." For instance, parochial schools in which thousands of children were educated under the watchful eye of the Catholic Church were replaced by a comprehensive education system controlled by the state; this change took place to, in turn, establish a new culture based on Marxist-Leninist precepts.[1] Cuban leaders utilized pedagogical strategies to foster the development of a new revolutionary conscience. From early on, various entities were created in order to put into practice the ideological conceptualization of the moment: the Cuban Film Institute (ICAIC), which produces and brings didactic documentaries, newsreels, and other films to the masses was created on March 24, 1959; the Organization of Pioneers and the system of educational scholarships for students of all ages, from young children to university students, was established; the Committees for the Defense of the Revolution (CDR) were founded to function at the neighborhood level, organizing the community in small sections in order to better

---

1. The Cuban leaders subscribe to the precepts established by Carl Marx and Vladimir Lenin. The former believed that a transformation of the economic system would produce cultural change. Lenin, however, argued that cultural change was only possible if intellectuals and leaders of the party molded the conscience of the masses (Gurley 72-74).

control the population,[2] and with the specific capacity to invade the private space of each citizen; the Literacy Campaign was organized in 1960 and was initiated one year later with the dispersal of the newly trained Volunteer Teachers to the most remote areas of the Island with the dual purpose of teaching reading and facilitating the inculcation of the new ideological thought; the Armed Forces (FAR) and the National Military were organized in 1960, replacing the previous military regime and the troops of the 26th of July Movement with young people trained under the new regime.

At the level of mass media, Radio Rebelde was inaugurated, a radio station that, during the years of the Sierra Maestra guerrilla warfare, served clandestinely to report insurgent activity. Also, the print press was officially organized under the shadow of the Journalism of the Revolutionary Front in March of 1961, along with the closing before June of 1960 of the newspapers *Diario de la marina, Prensa libre, El país,* and *Diario nacional y Excélsior,* all associated with the incumbent government, in order to make room for the dailies *Hoy, Revolución,* and later *Verde olivo, Trabajadores,* and *Granma,* among others. All of these mechanisms of ideological indoctrination were successful in the first ten years of the Revolution. However, beginning in the 1970s, the previous propaganda intensified and was accompanied by a greater degree of repression and censorship. In *Cuba: The Shaping of Revolutionary Consciousness* (1990), Tzvi Medin explains that the revolutionary government understood perfectly that different measures needed to be taken in order to supplant the initial and transitory euphoria, and thus the formulation and implementation of a new revolutionary conscience was indispensable:

> Castro conceived his political power in terms of strengthening the base of popular power, and he understood the need to

---

2. According to Julie Marie Bunck, "The government established the Committees for the Defense of the Revolution [CDR] as a system to mobilize and reeducate citizens, to publicize official goals and to promote and organize cooperatives, civil defense, and first-aid projects" (9).

perpetuate the base by developing a revolutionary consciousness in the masses to take place of merely transitory enthusiasm. (9)

By means of the diverse methods enumerated above, the Cuban government decreed from the outset what it means to be a *good revolutionary,* a concept to which all Cuban citizens would have to adhere in order to avoid alienation or repression. The strategy of the government, ironically imposed from the official pulpit, was based on the notion that each citizen should feel included in the decision-making process of the country; the revolutionary conscience was based on the conceptualization that "we" (together) are working towards the future of the nation, and thus the achievements or failures of the country were in the hands of the people rather than in those of the autocracy, who in reality were the ones who were making all of the resolutions without democratic consensus. This contradiction, along with the different coercive methods that always existed and that increased with time (such as the distinct levels of censorship: institutional, direct, indirect, self-censorship, labor sanctions, "acts of repudiation" in work, and study centers),[3] are all preponderant factors in the acceptance, for lack of another option, of the newly established politics by the majority of the Cuban population.

GAYS IN THE REVOLUTION

I have thus established that one of the explicit goals of the new government from the time of its inauguration in 1959 was to inculcate in all of its subjects new systems of thought, of action, of responding, and this I designate on the cognitive level *the* revolutionary conscience. As the explicit purpose of this chapter is to

---

3. The *actos de repudio* (acts of repudiation) were meetings presided over by Communist party leaders that were officially enacted in work and study centers with the express objective of renouncing the conduct of a colleague.

explore gay themes in Cuban literature, first I must attempt to respond to two basic questions, one of a general character, and one that pertains particularly to gays in Cuba. One must first consider gay identity is understood in general, and secondly, establish how the gay individual fits into the new rigorous parameters established by the Revolution and demanded of all citizens through revolutionary decree.[4]

I believe it is possible to argue that human beings are in an evolutionary process in which, as Jane Gallop asserts, identity "must be continually assumed and continually called into question" (cited in Weeks 69). In the specific terms of sexual identity, the power that the hegemonic heterosexual society exerts upon society as a whole assumes that its own standards are constants and that "normal" behavior is heterosexual. Thus, if an individual identifies him or herself publicly as homosexual, he or she runs the risk of being classified as an individual who deviates from the "norm," of being perverse or perverted. This entire game of power—of highly homophobic origin—has as its purpose "[to] obscure a real sexual diversity with the myth of a sexual destiny" (Weeks 74), and succeeds in limiting and compartmentalizing the individual vis-à-vis a theoretical basis of a theological, biological, and juridical nature. By preventing a group from recognizing itself and being accepted under the rubric of a union which defies the norm of sexual identity imposed upon society as a whole, the patriarchal hegemony successfully debilitates the unified resistance that a gay movement could exert. Moreover, a participant in gay resistance activism does not necessarily consider him or herself homosexual, but rather may identify with any group that is politically or

---

4. Throughout this study we use the term "gay" as a theoretico-cultural concept instead of the official term "homosexual," in an attempt to avoid any possible stereotype that is associated with the latter's medico-juridical classification. Furthermore, we do not refer to the parallel lesbian terms, since within the Cuban patriarchy such relations are not rejected; they are not deemed as a threat to the Cuban patriarchy, and thus do not form part of the revolutionary ethic/code of conduct.

ideologically oppressed by the majority in power. Gay resistance validates a sexual identity previously considered dissident, marginalized, and sworn to secrecy. As Weeks points out, in the case of the United States, San Francisco as a geographical location helps to organize and validate the sexual identity of a group of men and women by providing them with a place where their sexuality is validated. On a much smaller scale, gay bars, theaters, and cinemas in other cities create temporal spaces of belonging and acceptance.

Having said this, I now need to establish the way in which homosexuality figure into the revolutionary ideology. It would be impossible to treat this question lightly. Historically in Cuba, like in the majority of Latin America, direct repression of gays has been openly practiced; after all, from the declaration of independence to the end of the last century, the Island was subjected to the castrating yoke of successive dictatorial regimes in which the most "macho" forcefully seized the power to govern.[5] As an inevitable consequence, from the time of its inception, the Cuban revolutionary ideology has categorically rejected any dissident expression that does not adhere to its precepts, and thus, Cuban gays find themselves in the epicenter of a iron-handed official persecution, repression, and ridicule that has lasted more than two decades. In effect, in an escapist game with the intent to avoid the deliberate homophobia characteristic of the Revolution, Fidel Castro himself attributed anti gay sentiment expressed by his government to traditional Latin American *machismo* during a personal interview:

> *Machismo* is an historical and cultural tradition that dates back to who knows when ... I must tell you in all honesty that I have never shared those sentiments ... in spite of having grown up in

---

5. Cuban homophobia transcends temporal (pre/post Castro) and spatial (Havana/Miami) frontiers. The homosexual in Miami suffers the same affronts as those on the Island. This similarity has inspired a popular saying that the only thing Havana and Miami have in common is the explicit hatred and persecution that gays suffer in both places.

this same machista society. I believe that there could have been an era in which machismo was very powerful, but it was not a product of the Revolution, but rather of the social environment in which we live. We cannot speak of a time like the one you describe in your question, because in reality there never has been a persecution of homosexuals here.(quoted in Bardach 50)

However, in another interview conducted by Lee Lockwood in 1966 and cited by Ann Louise Bardach, Castro states explicitly that homosexuality is "a deviation of nature ... We could never come to believe that a homosexual would embody the conditions and conduct requirements that could permit us to consider him a true revolutionary"(50). These words, articulated by Castro in the middle of the repressive process of the camps of the Unidades Militares de Ayuda a la Producción [Military Units for the Aid of Production, (UMAP) which operated between 1965 and 1969], denote the tone of the official position taken against the sexual dissident during the 1960s, and that endures even now when the "homosexual condition" is still considered an impediment for the revolutionary citizen. This is exemplified by the fact that membership in the exclusive Cuban Communist Party, sole guide for the political direction of the country, is explicitly prohibited to homosexuals.

However, I must clarify that, in continuing with the *machista*-patriarchal Latin American tradition, in Cuba a man is not categorized as homosexual for maintaining sexual relations with another man: "to have sex with another man is not what identifies one as a homosexual. For many Cubans, a man is homosexual only if he takes the passive receiving role.... A man is suspected of being a homosexual only if his behavior is not macho" (Leinier 22). A similar example of this erroneous conceptualization of gay identity can be found, in a conversation that took place in Havana during the summer of 1994. Juan Nicolás Padrón, then editor in chief of the publishing house Letras Cubanas, discussed the topic when asked about the discrimination that Reinaldo Arenas suffered during his pilgrimage through Cuba:

Look, Reinaldo Arenas was an individual who no one liked because of one simple reason, because in the middle of a *machista* society like ours, like all of the rest of Latin American society, a person who wore flowered pants, sandals and who proclaimed his homosexuality was a shocking individual. Here, in the Vatican, in the United States, if apart from the fact that you are a declared homosexual, you also are a man who publicly announces your total disaffection, then it shouldn't surprise you that you're already looking for trouble. (Alvarez 140)

From the start, then, with its patriarchal inheritance, the Revolution assumes compulsory heterosexual practices. David William Foster explains that from its inception, the Cuban Marxist-Leninist dogmatism rejecting gay culture was:

[no] other than one of bourgeois capitalism's many diseased faces, and its failure to distinguish between homosexuality (particularly as it was viewed and consumed by the foreign tourist in Havana) as part of the corrupt market system and gay identity as a dimension of personal liberation, provided a potent substratum for homophobia of the Castro Revolution. (*Sexual Textualities* 88)

I share Foster's assertion and concur that gay identity is a dimension of personal freedom, and therefore, there is no doubt that this concept is diametrically opposed to the absolute uniformity and conformity that the Revolution has always demanded of all of its citizens. In other words, here I am referring to the imposition of a so-called revolutionary identity a priori that is necessarily prejudiced and exclusive. To bring the discussion from the particular case in question to a more general level, one can make use of Diana Fuss's conceptualization of "political identity": "identity is always purchased at the price of the exclusion of the Other, the repression or repudiation of nonidentity" (103).

Also, one must not forget that, in its most general sense, the persecution of homosexuals coincides with the persecution of the dissident: a homosexual is a dissident of the bourgeois norm of conjugal life. When the role "revolutionary Man," that has been autocratically designated, is transgressed, the power that the heterosexual hegemony attributes to itself is violated; this violation evokes a counterattack by hegemonic reactionary forces which, besides being repressive and controlling, violently lash out upon perceiving that the sexual order is being challenged. In the Cuban case in particular—whose socialist society has perpetuated bourgeois relations among heterosexual partners—the official responses were multiple, but for the most part, at the start of the 1960s, they took the form of indiscriminate arrests and subsequent transfers of citizens (all men suspected of being homosexual) to the UMAP camps.[6] Lamentably, many Cuban intellectuals suffered imprisonment in these work camps. Among the most renowned were the writer Reinaldo Arenas[7] (1943-90), the poet and director of the publishing house El Puente, (an independent organ of literary dissemination from 1961-1964); José Mario, the poet Jorge Ronet and the actor Rafael Polet.[8] In 1971, the First National Congress of Education and Culture took place, and the repression persisted even though the UMAP camps had disappeared years before. The Congressional resolutions, which are of particular importance for this study are the ones which refer to homosexuality, since, for the first time, an official document did not allude to homosexuality in criminal terms, but rather in medical and psychological ones. The resolutions continued to be drastic for gays in that they called for their prohibition from educational forums, which increased intellectual and political discrimination. Extracts from the multiple resolutions were printed in diverse mass media publications such as *Casa de las Américas*, *Granma*, and

---

6. It is estimated that before the dismantling of UMAP camps in December of 1969, more than 35,000 homosexuals, religious followers (primarily Jehovah's witnesses), and those deemed "counter-revolutionaries" suffered mandatory sentences there.

7. In his novel *Arturo la estrella más brillante* (1984), Arenas fictionalizes much of his experiences in the UMAP camps.

8. See the film *Conducta impropia* (Improper Conduct; 1984).

Unión. In the following excerpt, I cite some of the passages that repudiate gay participation in cultural and educational revolutionary life:[9]

> The resolution was reached that flamboyant homosexuals must not be permitted to exert influence over our youth using the justification of "artistic merit."/ Therefore, we call for a decision regarding how to confront the homosexual presence in the diverse institutions of our cultural sector./ Cultural forums cannot serve as a frame for the proliferation of false intellectuals that seek to convert [...] homosexuality and other social aberrations, into expressions of revolutionary art, alienated from the masses and from the spirit of our Revolution. ("Declarations" 5)

Nonetheless, although in the 1970s Cuba perpetuated the hegemony of a patriarchal and compulsory heterosexual society—evident, for example, in the demographics of the Politburó in the last thirty-four years[10]—the leaders officially tried to promote certain changes. In 1974, the Family Code which "eliminates" the double work day for women, obliging men to share the housework, was approved. Likewise, in 1977, the National Cuban Group for Sex Education was created and directed by the Cuban medical doctor Celestino Lajonchere in collaboration with the German sexologist Monika Krause. This group, in conjunction with other entities for health education, is dedicated to the study and promotion of information relevant to sexuality, thus promoting a certain degree of instruction previously unavailable to the masses. On the other hand, the Penal Code was established in 1978—that is, towards the end of the *Decenio Negro* (Black Decade) in Cuban

---

9. These quotes were taken from *Granma Weekly Review,* the English edition of the official newspaper of the Cuban Communist Party, from May 9, 1971.

10. In 1975, Carlos Montaner points out that in that era, of the one hundred members comprising the Politburo, the Secretariat and the Central Committee of the Communist Party, only five were women.

culture. Although it provides a certain degree of flexibility in differentiating between homosexual expression in the public and private space, it puts severe restrictions on the cultural production of gay themes and content (Citron 39). For instance, a documentary about the painter René Portocarrero, filmed under the auspices of the ICAIC, omits the fact that the famous artist is gay, and one of the few able to maintain an openly gay lifestyle in Cuba due to his internationally renowned cultural work and contributions.

In *The Cultural Revolution in Cuba* (1991), Roger Reed adds that, along general lines, Castro's government accosted the gay citizenry of Cuba because "[H]omosexuals are rebels; they dissent from conventional morality. Therefore, they pose a challenge to any system in which all modes of behavior are supposed to be controlled by the authorities" (80). That is to say, gays do not conform to moralizing rules and laws; to put it in the vocabulary used in this study, gays articulate one of the most irreverent forms of contestatory expression. Therefore, to reinforce Foster's assertion, because gay culture was viewed as the remains of bourgeois capitalism in the initial years of the Revolution in Cuba, a hyper-masculinization of a society established on the basis of an evolving nationalist socialism was carried out. The most obvious modification could be observed in the physical appearance of the revolutionaries: the long locks sported by the Sierra rebels were replaced with Prussian haircuts that the recruits of the subsequent Fuerzas Armadas Revolucionarias [(FAR) Revolutionary Armed Forces] began to wear. In turn, the "masculine" olive green uniforms of the campaigns began to be worn by the female militant revolutionaries. These stylistic changes were one more way of putting into practice the conceptualization of the "New Man" who, according to Che Guevara, should rise up from the revolutionary process.[11]

---

11. Montaner states with justifiable conviction: "Guevara was the first, the last, and the only New Man that the revolutionary process created. The disinterested, hard-working, honest, critical, future Cuban

For all intents and purposes, then, the only option for (intellectual) gays striving to survive in their country was self-censorship, that is, forcibly silencing their identities upon realizing that the hegemonic powers were too mighty to defeat or even to persuade. Lourdes Argüelles and Ruby Rich accurately assert that Cuban intellectual gays of the 1960s and 1970s did not organize any type of unified internal resistance that would permit them to counter the governmental assault. The aforementioned authors attribute the lack of opposition to three fundamental factors: (1) at the beginning of the 1960s, Cuba lacked a discursive feminist tradition, impeding the establishment of a base from which to discuss sexual hierarchy or gender politics; (2) the contemporary mind set did not allow for a vision much beyond the notion that homosexuality was practiced in sinister places with limited or no sexual implications; (3) many intellectuals feared the loss of privileges-the most valued of this being trips abroad that permitted them the freedom to explore their sexual orientation-if they vocalized their opinions against the official position regarding homosexuality (691).

I have already mentioned various young intellectuals who suffered internment in the UMAP camps after having been arbitrarily identified as "homosexuals." However, there are others who, due to their intellectual maturity and international fame, could not be openly oppressed like their novice counterparts were. One case in particular involves the narrator and playwright Virgilio Piñera (1912-1979), who, by the time of the triumph of the Revolution, was already a recognized figure in literary circles for having published the novel *La carne de René* (1952), the short stories collection *Cuentos fríos* (1956), and dramatic works such as *Electra Garrigó, Jesús,* and *Aire frío* (1959).[12] Like many other

---

was [Che] himself; 70).

12. Piñera also formed part of the exclusive group of contributors to the journal *Orígenes.* Immediately after it went out of print, he founded the journal *Ciclón* with José Rodríguez Feo. According to Reinaldo Arenas, the latter was "another journal much more irreverent than the first, practically a homosexual one, and all under Batista's reactionary

intellectuals, in 1959, Piñera jumped on the revolutionary bandwagon and contributed to the pages of the magazine *Revolución* and the literary supplement *Lunes*, but his decadence began at the moment he was arrested and imprisoned in El Morro[13] in October, 1961. From this point on, Virgilio Piñera would suffer from an internal exile that would last until his death. The only alternative left to him was to exercise a silence that would permit his survival. In the intriguing essay, "Fleshing Out Virgilio Piñera from the Cuban Closet" (1995), José Quiroga comments on the possible reasons for Piñera's silence: "depending on your political point of view, this was the silence of fear, of repression, of inner exile, the silence of the literary closet and of the refusal to come out of that closet or perhaps this was the silence of the heroic" (170). It is true that Piñera was able to publish three works at the end of the 1960s: the novel *Presiones y diamantes* (1967), the play *Dos viejos pánicos* (1968), and a collection of poems entitled *La vida entera* (1969). However, after this last publication, on the eve of the Stalinist Gray Quinquennium, Piñera was forced into literary silence until his death. Knowing the irreverent character of Virgilio Piñera (gay, anti-Communist, anti-Catholic), one must agree with Quiroga's final estimation of this author as heroically silent, and I would add that silence is one of the few expressions of resistance that could be practiced in Cuba in the 1970s. However, Reinaldo Arenas observes in his autobiography, *Antes que anochezca* (1992), that Piñera, from the closet, directly influenced subsequent generations by serving as their mentor:

> I used to visit Virgilio Piñera at home at seven in the morning ... sitting in front of me, he read a copy of the novel [*El mundo*

bourgeois dictatorship. The first thing Virgilio did was publish the Marquis de Sade's *The One Hundred and Twenty Days of Sodom and Gomorra"* 106).

13. This is the same prison in which his disciple, Reinaldo Arenas, would be incarcerated for eighteen months after being sentenced in 1974.

alucinante] and where he thought that I should add a comma or change one word for another, he told me so ... He was my university professor as well as my friend.(105)

I cannot conclude this section without first mentioning that the homophobic posture and the repressive measures that the Revolution assumed went beyond its own citizens. For example, the North American poet Allen Ginsberg was thrown out of Cuba in 1965, after having been invited to participate as a judge of the Casa de las Américas poetry prize that same year, for protesting against gay persecution. Upon his return to the United States, Ginsberg admitted that the worst thing he said in Cuba was that Raúl Castro was gay[14] and that Che Guevara was very beautiful (quoted in Reed 82); of course, with this comments, he struck at the heterosexual *machista* heart of the Revolution.

THREE GENERATIONS OF HOMOEROTIC WRITING IN CUBA

Homoerotic writing is not a foreign genre to Cuban literature. In 1928, the novel *Angel de Sodoma* was published in Madrid by the Cuban Alfonso Hernández Catá, a text that portrays the protagonist, José María, first born of the Vélez Gomara family, as a confused individual who finds himself forced into fighting against his distinct homoerotic inclinations. These "tendencias" [tendencies] are justified by the narrator, following the Spanish tradition of the era—as in the case of Gregorio Marañón—by presenting them as accidents of nature: "What fault is it of mine? ... If Nature, or God, or Satan were going to make me a woman and, when the seeds of my being were already planted, they

---

14. Ginsberg makes reference to a rumor circulating for many years. It was not uncommon to hear that the second in command of the Revolution was seen frequenting gay hangouts such as El Floridita and Las Casa de las Infusiones.

changed their minds and in bad faith they threw in clay belonging to men, what am I to do? " (84).

José María's dilemma is a vivid historical representation of the gay individual's entrapment in the codes of a patriarchal society. Throughout his life, he is forced to assume a social identity that goes against not only his sexual desire, but also against the person that he is, and that obliges him to identify with those masculine values and repress his "lado femenino" (feminine side) in order to "absorber" (absorb) the masculinity of his father (85). Likewise, he submits himself to changing his physical appearance into a "masculine" one, despite the fact that this tramples his personal integrity. These practices range from a "violento" (violent) exercise regime that he completes daily (98) to hardening his soft skin by exposing it to an abusive sun "that burned his hide, produced tremendous blisters and left a sparking of caustic, terrible little stars in his eyes" (98-99). The protagonist convinces himself of the possibility of "regenerarse" (redemption) in the public space by means of marriage and fatherhood, confirmed by what he reads in "a science book" that he had consulted "one time, with shame and terror, [in] the Municipal Library" (137). "That's where the ultimate salvation forever is" (136). "A son that he would not raise in the folds of his mother's skirts, like he was raised; a son who instead of playing with dolls and hanging around with girls, would be continually in the sun, among mischievous boys, even when he would return with bumps and blisters!" (137).

In the pages of *Angel de Sodoma,* the reader cannot ignore the reality that discourages the protagonist throughout his life. Parisian exile and the subsequent suicide that ends José María's life are the only options open to him as a gay man who, after endless pondering, cannot deny his gay identity, and even less, can maintain a farce in order to placate the demands of society. It is important to note that the end of this novel satisfies the patriarchal perspective, since it results in the of homosexual's extermination, the explicit goal of compulsory heterosexuality.

Some ten years after the publication of Hernández Catá's novel, the, narrator and journalist Carlos Montenegro wrote the novel *Hombres sin mujer* (1937) in Cuba, a work which closely links homosexuality to violence by portraying the discrimination and exercise of power over the weak in the daily routine among common prisoners in Cuban jails during that era.[15] Unlike the previously discussed novel, *Hombres sin mujer* is a cruel and disturbing autobiography, full of sex from start to finish, in which *bugarronería* (anal penetration of one man by another, the latter performing the "feminine" role of receiver) is the law of prison life.[16] However, like *Angel de Sodoma*, the tragic ending that characterizes canonical Western writing cannot be escaped in this work either. Montenegro writes the prologue to the novel himself, and in it, he informs the reader that his work is highly testimonial, and he makes clear that his purpose is "denouncing of a prison system to which he found himself subjected for twelve years" at the same time, he does not make any sort of apology to those who might consider the content immoral since "everything the [pages]

---

15. In the entry that Alfredo Villanueva writes about Carlos Montenegro in *Latin American Writers on Gay and Lesbian Themes: A Bio-Critical Source Book,* he accurately point out that *Hombres sin mujer* resembles Adolfo Caminha's novel *Bom-Crioulo (*1895) in that it presents a homoerotic relationship between a black man (strong and older) and a white boy (weak and young) which terminates in the death of both protagonists because of jealousy towards a third party. The critic argues that *Othello* is the model for this type of writing which treats interracial relations between protagonists and ends in tragedy: "Thus one may venture the hypothesis that in relationships between whites and members of any other racial group, the expected outcome is rupture, separation and personal tragedy for both partners, or at least the nonwhite partner irrespective of the gender of the individuals concerned" (250).

16. This work by Montenegro anticipates the theme of the prison in connection with homosexuality that will later be addressed by the narrations of other authors: José María Arguedas, *El sexto* (1961); Manuel Puig, *El beso de la mujer araña (*1976). In 1966, the Chilean writer José Donoso published his novel *El lugar sin límites (*1965) which is the story of La Manuela, a transvestite protagonist. However unlike the novels already mentioned, he does so openly.

say correspond to an existing evil" (7). In this case, this evil does not refer to the same-sex relations themselves that take place in the jails, but rather the violence which one is capable of perpetrating against another human being in order to derive erotic pleasure.

The novel is told in the third person by an ubiquitous narrator who frequently appears in the text itself. The physical space of the narration is the closed setting of the prison, yet the characters appear in different situations in distinct spaces: the bathroom, the galley, the infirmary, their respective cells, the patio, and the workroom. Although time in the novel is linear, the narrator interrupts the chronology with flashbacks that inform the reader of previous occurrences, and the narration seems to be circular as well, since at the end of the text crazy Valentín yells out the same words that he says at the beginning of the novel, " I want to eat white chicken!" (11, 216).

The protagonist of *Hombres sin mujer* is Pascasio Speek, a black Cuban who has served eight years of a prison term for having stabbed a man who attempted to rape him. The text is very explicit in presenting the psychological changes which haunt the protagonist, whose greatest worry is to maintain an impeccable record of conduct in order to get out of jail as soon as possible. Initially, he cannot understand why one man would carry on sexual relations with another, and therefore, he rejects the possibility of entering into any such situation, forcing himself to satisfy his sexual urges through masturbation:

> How is it possible that one man can propose to make another fall in love with him? ... He had ended up laughing himself to hysterics .... Come on! He also possessed the means.... And blood.... And power .... And ... lightning! ... But, when he was really desperate, he dreamed of Encarnación, of Tomasa, with whatever broomstick was around, but with skirts, and ready, on to the next one!(15)

During the eight years he spends in prison, Pascasio does not merely reject such homoerotic practices on an abstract level, but rather, when La Morita tries to force him into having sex, Pascasio gives him a ferocious beating: "Pascasio Speek gave him a punch right in the face, and as he was still close enough since the others were holding [La Morita] up, he bit him again with fury until [La Morita] was rolling around on the floor with his face full of blood" (42). However, as the story progresses, the reader comes to realize that Pascasio's explicit homophobia stems from his fear of his attraction to the same sex and that this is a desire that goes beyond a simple sexual need. At the same time, as the novel advances, the narration overturns the initial conception that sex between men is "anormal" (abnormal) (16) or perverse: "Do you know what the deal is with all of us?" Matienzo asks the recently jailed Andrés. "It's that we are men without women! There are no perverts here; only men without women.... That's all" (56), and it reinforces the concept that homoeroticism does not take the manliness out of a man:

You're crazy, but. . . .

[Andrés] couldn't finish his sentence; Pascasio's arm had encircled him and brought him closer to himself, confusing their two mouths. Andrés did not put up any sort of a fight; he closed his eyes, abandoning himself, until Pascasio, astounded by what he himself was doing, let [Andrés] go. Then the boy repeated what he had begun to say to him: "You're crazy, but you're a man...(152)

The erotic-love relationship that Pascasio and Andrés establish in the course of the novel reproduces those of heterosexual relations. In particular, there is the question of jealousy, which leads to Andrés' murder and Pascasio's suicide after the latter finds his lover in the workshop in Manuel Chiquito's company:

Andrés, with his pants unzipped, ran towards Pascasio and was about to tell him something, but he didn't have time: he stopped all of a sudden, with broken words in his throat and eyes wet with tears looking at Pascasio, who had dug the cutting edge of a key into [Andrés'] cranium with all the might of his arm and of his savagery. (214)

Cuban narrative had to wait until after the triumph of the Revolution in 1959 for the theme of homosexuality to present itself in another novel, in this case, *Paradiso* (1966), considered to be the masterpiece of poet, narrator and essayist José Lezama Lima (1910-76). It is well known that the historical context in which this novel was published was precisely one of relentless discrimination against homosexuals. This was the apex of the UMAP camps years (1965-69); it is estimated that thousands of gays—and those arbitrarily designated as such for having long hair or walking a particular way or, for other whims of the homophobic military and police—were sent to these camps.[17] Also, it is during these years that the government dismantled the independent editorial group El Puente, and its director, José Mario, along with other members, was sent to the UMAP camps. During the First Congress of Education and Culture in 1971, the Cuban government adopted the official stance of openly rejecting gays; in cultural and educational spheres they were altogether excluded.

Within this historical Cuban context, *Paradiso* appeared seven years after Batista's fall, a time when the aureola of initial enthusiasm was being put to the test by the fights in the Escambray mountains, the exile or death of some of the pioneers of the Revolution who fought alongside Fidel in the Sierra Maestra. There was also a subtle disenchantment and internal opposition, including the exile of well-known intellectuals who had at first collaborated on the reforms. In terms of literature in particular, the year that this work appeared is of specific importance because it marks the beginning of what will later come to be known as Golden Quinquennium of the Cuban short story, inaugurated by

---

17. See the documentary *Conducta impropia,* in which various individuals interviewed elaborate in detail the selective proceedings used by state security agencies to arrest young people who would later be sent to the UMAP camps.

Jesús Díaz's prize-winning collection of stories Los *años duros* (1966). It is important to note that, until this time, almost all of the works published in Cuba, exalted the Revolution one way or another. It is in the atmosphere of tension between the historical moment and the literary production that had been published up until this moment that *Paradiso* appeared, a work of profound universal content that did not pay any attention whatsoever to the historical events that had transpired in Cuba during the five years previous to its publication. In other words, with *Paradiso,* Lezama Lima, instead of reflecting on the history that circumscribed his era, mentioning names, events, or nationalist/pseudopatriotic examples, drew references from the Bible, the Asians, the Romans, the Egyptians, and from Greek mythology. Socratic thought, which sees the world as something larger than a simple and tangible reality, consistently runs through the works of Lezama Lima:

> According to Lezama, it is a matter of looking for the absolute and the comprehension of the world beyond appearances. Such thinking reveals that the writer is confident in the existence of a reality hidden behind the appearances of the physical world. Consequently, a constant feature in his essays is the search for concealed connections and unexpected linkings that move away from the linearity of rationalistic thought. (Altamiranda 203)

In addition to the hermetism and the apparent verbal obscurity with which Lezama Lima writes (circumlocution, periphrases, prosopopoeia—all elements that form part of the narrative technique of baroque writing), it is also important to note his great literary license which does not limit itself to set structures, and juxtaposes narratives that have no outward relation, giving the readers the impression that at times they face a block of pages lacking a common thread. As the Argentine writer Julio Cortázar— one of the first to write about *Paradiso* in the same year as its publication[18]—says, the novel works on different levels, from familiar narrations to which we easily relate, to erotic and imaginary ones that border on magical/fantastic literature. In reference to the characters of *Paradiso,* Cortázar comments that we have to take into account that all of them are viewed in "esencia" (essence) rather than "presencia" (presence); they are archetypes, not types. We have to accept that these characters present themselves and speak from the "imagen" (image) cloistered in the Lezamian poetic system. The characters themselves are not important for Lezama, rather what is crucial is the complete mystery that encloses human experience (137-44).

The novel is divided into three parts, connected by the events in the life of the protagonist, José Cemí, and more specifically, his awakening to his sexual identification. In the first section (chapters one to six), the narrator focuses on providing the ancestral history of the Cemí family. In the next section (chapters eight to eleven), the narrator presents the protagonist's adolescent years in high school and college. In these candid passages, Cemí's philosophical and sexual initiation in the company of his classmates Fronesis and Foción is portrayed. In the rest of the novel, the text first presents four dreams that the protagonist experiences (chapter twelve) and the work concludes with the introduction and development of the character Oppiano Licario (13-14), who becomes Cemí's "*lazarillo*" (person who guides the blind) during the last years of his philosophical formation, and who provides the title for Lezama's last work, which he never finished due to his death.

In Cuba in the mid-1960's, when cultural politicking started to become institutionalized, and no one cared to make the distinction between politics and aesthetics, one of the errors[19] that Lezama

---

18. The essay cited here originally appeared in the journal *Unión* 4 (1966): 36-60.

19. Due to Lezama Lima's international status, the Stalinist-Cuban censorship could not penalize him to the same degree as it would later do so with Reinaldo Arenas and Heberto Padilla. However, his literary audacity cost him the strictest limit on the copies of his novel (only 4,000

Lima made with his publication of *Paradiso* was to neglect any credit or reference to the revolutionary process.[20] Furthermore, and in direct relation to this study, the Cuban writer did not only allude to and present homoerotic space (along with heterosexual, incestuous, voyeuristic, adulterous, exhibitionist, and sadomasochistic spaces), but rather more importantly, in my opinion, he did so on the same level as heterosexual eroticism, thus validating that which the Revolution—and the patriarchal hegemony itself—attempted to punish. This is to say that, seen in my analysis of chapter 8, the narration does not concern itself with making gender distinctions between the two bodies that make love. However, in terms of the entirety of the novel, I agree with the Cuban-American critic Gustavo Pérez Firmat who proposes that the main protagonist's "attainment of Paradise entails a concomitant affirmation of his homosexuality" (247).[21]

---

printings were allowed) and the repeated rejection of his applications to leave the country, despite frequent invitations from abroad.

20. Lezama Lima never took a directly antagonistic stance against the Revolution. In fact, he was one of the intellectuals who initially supported its cultural direction; in January of 1959 he signed, along with other intellectuals, a public document supporting the Revolution; in 1960 he is named Director of Literature and Publications of the Dirección Nacional de Cultural [National Agency for Culture]; and in 1961 he was elected as one of six vice-presidents of the Cuban Writers and Artists Union, under the leadership of the poet Nicolás Guillén. Recently, *La gaceta de Cuba* published a letter written by Lezama to Fidel Castro on February 1, 1959, in which this great master of letters expressed gratitude towards the revolutionaries for their efforts: "You, sir, have sown the tree of Liberty with roots firmly and powerfully planted in the fertile terrain of public conscience (quoted in Bianchi 18).

21. Pérez Firmat argues that José Cemí's sexual position is, up to the end of the novel, quite undecided, almost androgenous. If it is true that his homosexuality is ambiguous, it is also true that he does not establish any heterosexual relations, even though he does have visions and erotic dream about his mother, dolphins, etc. Pérez Firmat contends that with Cemí's descent into "las profundidades" (the depths), the last scene of the novel

The chapter in question could very well have the title, "Sex: presence and reality in human beings." This estimation diametrically opposes the commentary that José Prats Sariol makes in the critical edition to *Paradiso,* edited by Cintio Vitier, and the one to which I make reference in this work, when he writes about chapter 8: "If we read carefully the respective descriptions, we can note that sense of bestiality envelops homosexual sex acts, whereas a festive, almost comical, sense surrounds the heterosexual ones." (662). A detailed comparison reveals that in this chapter, for example, the narrator presents a total of five erotic episodes which include sexual intercourse: three are heterosexual and two are homosexual encounters. These latter are preceded and complemented by a passage in which the narrator describes an occasion in which one of the students, Leregas, brags publicly in geography class about his "phallic potency which reigns like Aaron's rod," causing the narrator to affirm that: "His very large penis was the geography class" (200). During the (doubly) pedagogic session and under the attentive eyes of fifty or sixty classmates, the narrator tells us: "Leregas revealed his penis and testicles, acquiring with only one single impetus the transformation of his genitals into a column of exceptional size." (201). In the page that precedes this description, the narrator explains:

> Leregas exposed his penis, with the same majestic indifference contained in the Velázquez painting in which the key is given over and placed on the pillow, at first, as small as a thimble, but afterwards, impelled like a titanical wind, it achieved the length of a manual laborer's forearm." (200)

I repeat that, in the images represented by the narrative text, there does not exist any indication that might suggest some type of jest or degradation. On the contrary, the group of spectators that:

---

fixes his acceptance of his homosexual desire.

> contemplated Leregas's defiance with—that tenacious cereus ready to break its wrapping at any moment, with an extremely polished blood-red helmet—which—magnetized with even more force the attentive curiosity of those frozen pilgrims ... but without any sarcasm nor mocking little grins. (201)

is formed by young people that, like José Cemí, are in a process of sexual self-discovery, of self-definition where sexual curiosity is not biased by any homophobic expression characteristic of patriarchal society. Indeed, this scene can be read as a utopic Lezamian configuration that refutes the analysis of Prats Sariol.

I have mentioned that in this chapter, over a period of three consecutive Sundays, five distinct episodes of sexual intercourse take place with Farraluque—the other character possessing sexual prowess—as the main protagonist. Farraluque's erotic encounters, treated all on the same semantic level, sustain my previous statement. Supporting Pérez Firmat's previously cited stance, the Argentine critic Daniel Altamiranda affirms that in those prolonged descriptive sequences, "the narrator establishes a principle of social behavior that seems omnipresent in Lezama Lima's universe: sexual indefinition as a distinctive factor in adolescence" (207). The first two erotic encounters that Farraluque has are heterosexual, with the director's cook and the maid on the first Sunday. The reader is told that his youth permits him "once he was finished with the normal intercourse [with the cook], he could then begin another *per angostam viam.*" (204). The next Sunday, Farraluque has his first homoerotic encounter after going to bed with "the woman [who] lived across the street," an episode that is distinct from "his two previous encounters which had been rough and clumsy, because now he was entering into the kingdom of subtlety and of diabolical specialization" (207). Afterwards, he has a sexual experience with Adolfito, known as *el miquito* (the little monkey), the cook's brother, and it is this character with whom Farraluque begins what could be called an erotic game of intense seduction between two bodies; here one enters into what the narrator designates "the kingdom of subtlety." The

Farraluque-Adolfito encounter is one of extreme refinement; the archaic schema "passive-active," or the possession of one (female-weak) by another (male-strong), has no resonance whatsoever in this description. The mutual pleasure between two bodies that is portrayed is an exemplary image of what Foster calls "two bodies that love each other," and, as Altamiranda articulates in the aforementioned quote, the universe of Lezamian sexual indefinition, concomitant with the utter lack of homophobic prejudice, permits the narrator to express sexual curiosity and to enjoy both bodies in the same way that he had during the descriptions of heterosexual coitus:

> when Farraluque tried to take aim, he twisted away from the serpent's path, and when, with his stinger he was determined to tease the other's penis from its hiding place, the latter would roll over again, with the promise of a calmer harbor for his prow. (207)

As noted, Farraluque is interested in establishing something that goes far beyond a mere sexual satisfaction on his part, a sexual schema much more common in Latin American literature—such as in Montenegro's novel, for example. The previous passage presents a scene of mutual eroticism and pleasure, in which Farraluque wants to share the erect penis of the opposite body, while the latter eroticizes the experience more by rotating his body and concealing his penis.

Paradiso is one of the first works (and one of the only ones) in Latin American literature in which a preconception of what it is like, or what it should be like, to be gay does not exist; that is, it does not contain a biased perspective in regard to homoeroticism. In his novel, Lezama Lima leads the reader through an oscillation of episodes, some humorous, others dramatic, in which he portrays the crises which affect a human being—any human—in the search for a personal sexual identity. Such an interwoven baroque work ends with the hopeful words, "we can begin"; José Cemí's life, for all of its sexual dichotomies, has yet to begin.

90.00 Amba (+)

40. hair
10 - floor
20 cash
11 cat food
22 Kroger
15 Pharmacy

117.00 + 90 =
207

9 10

The official attitude that created a climate of extreme oppression towards any dissidence persisted and intensified throughout the 1970s (the Black Decade, as the critic Ambrosio Fornet christened), which were crucial years in the intellectual formation of writers born between 1950 and 1958, such as Francisco López Sacha, Leonardo Padura Fuentes, and Senel Paz, and those of the *Novísima* generation, born between 1959 and 1972, as I discussed in previous chapters.

As I write these lines, I find myself in the middle of an *ajiaco* of contradictions, as Gustavo Pérez Firmat would say. Initial readings of short stories written and published in Cuba during the last ten years, can, at first glance, seem like texts that transgress the habitual politico-ideological parameters inscribed within the historico-social dialect of the Cuban Revolution; however, this reading is contradicted upon a second reading. Among other elements I find the strong homophobic sentiment that has flourished in Latin American countries, and overall in the first three decades of the Cuban revolutionary process. I am referring specifically to the stories "El cazador" (1991) by the fiction writer-journalist Leonardo Padura Fuentes, and to the already very famous short story by Senel Paz, *El lobo, el bosque y el hombre nuevo* (1990), the latter serving as the basis for the screenplay of the film, *Fresa y chocolate* (1993). It is important to note that both works were winners of literary prizes in México and the film was nominated for Hollywood's Oscar for best foreign film of 1995. Also, the first story won an honorary mention in *Plural* magazine's literary contest in 1990, and the second received the prestigious Juan Rulfo award in the same year. However, if I submit these narrations to a second, more mature reading, I conclude that my first estimation has been hasty. In retrospect, my error can be attributed to, among other factors, the incorporation into the plot of the character of the "other," which leads the studious reader of Cuban literary production towards the discovery of a theme not previously explored. That is to say, the subject in Senel Paz's short story who declares himself homosexual and Catholic, but also a revolutionary with conviction, who jumped on the progressive revolutionary train by participating in the Literacy Campaigns of the 1960s, captures the imagination of the reader by presenting a perspective which is, to a certain extent, critical of the Revolution. Therefore, it is easy to conclude that the aforementioned text portrays a social judgment previously veiled or nonexistent, and is thus a progressive text in the politico-ideological field. However, once the story is deconstructed, the reader realizes something very evident; what strives to be a vanguard text is, in reality, a textually homophobic representation from the very same character who openly declares himself homosexual and who, of course, authorizes the rhetoric. Furthermore, I suggest that this novella, and later the script for the film as well, once again reproduces the cultural proposals of the heterosexual bourgeois society mimesis of Castro's Cuba where expressions distinct from those practiced by the hegemonic culture have always been marginalized or punished.

My second readings have followed Gloria Anzaldúa's arguments suggested in her article, "To(o) Queer the Writer: loca, escritora y chicana" (1991). Anzaldúa suggests that the reader should read with what she calls "facultad" (257); that is to say, one should read with the intent "to 'see into' and 'see through' unconscious falsifying disguises by penetrating the surface and reading underneath the words and between the lines" (238). In other words, my work has taken the form of a contestatory reader who, according to what Alberto Julián Pérez writes "criticizes the authority of the hegemonic model that seeks to inculcate itself and its vision of the world which this model transmits and strives to legitimate "(287).

My purpose in this segment is twofold: first, as I previously mentioned, I have attempted to present a reading that goes beyond a primary or superficial analysis motivated by pseudointellectual sentiment; secondly, and perhaps most crucially, I wish to highlight the literary criticism interested in the specific component of queer themes in recent Cuban narrative, which is difficult to locate in libraries, as this body of criticism has been only fragmentarily published in Cuba and/or abroad. I do this in hopes of promoting a genuine, enriching dialogue.

After the debut of *Paradiso*, it is not until the publication of the short story "¿Por qué llora Leslie Caron?" (1988) by Roberto Urías that a text appears in Cuba whose central theme is the dilemma of a gay character. In 1986, Urias's story won a national prize for literature, and it was published for the first time in the journal *Letras cubanas* in 1988, twenty two years after the publication of Lezama Lima's novel.[22] Even though it is the first short story that revisits the theme of the homosexual in the Revolution, a motif begun by Lezama Lima, Virgilio Piñera, and Reinaldo Arenas[23] among others, Uría's story is the most humane of its contemporaries in that it presents a nonhomophobic vision, one that is not biased against the gay individual in the post-revolutionary Cuban society. The protagonist, Francisco, defines his own identity by declaring that he prefers the name "Leslie Caron," since "my pals admit that she, the actress, and I have a lot in common; we have the same grace and the same ethereal air." (236). Through the voice of this gay character, the author both deconstructs the hegemonic heterosexual parameters of bourgeois society that have been reproduced in Castroist Cuba, and satirizes the trite and tired Marxist-Leninist rhetoric. At the start of the story, the protagonist admits to having a "sacred" family: "a mother, a father, an adorable little sister, a dog and lots of plants ... the classic decorous and decorated nest" (236). Thus, he refers to the scenario of the supposedly perfect heterosexual bourgeois existence. Nevertheless, what is presented initially as the ideal is, in reality, a satire of a deplorable situation: a father who keeps mistresses and never remembers his children's birthdays, a mother who leaves the house to put an end to her sorrows, and a

---

22. According to a comment made by Francisco López Sacha in *La Gaceta de Cuba* (marzo-abril 1993): 43, in 1984, the *Novísimo* writer Miguel Mejides published a lesbian short story entitled "Mi prima Amanda" in the journal *Bohemia*. I have not, unfortunately, been able to locate this text, in part due to the lack of an index for this journal.

23. His fiction with the exception of *Celestino antes del alba* (1967), is published in its entirety abroad and therefore I do not address it here.

sister who "marries some guy just because he has a house in Miramar and a car and a VCR" (238). In this short story, unlike others that treat gay themes (such as the one by Senel Paz), the protagonist has his own legitimate voice and in no way needs to perform self-criticism nor apologize for his gay identity. Rather, from his position outside the heterosexist hegemony, the protagonist is better able to critique those he observes: "the majority of people are pitiful; they are empty, and so false; they move only within the narrow limits of the paradigms imposed upon them" (238). Here, he describes the heterosexual world that surrounds him.

If it is true that El *lobo, el bosque y el hombre nuevo* (1990) and *Fresa y chocolate* (1993) are texts which advocate tolerance towards the Other in an oppressive and intransigent society, as both the film's director Tomás Gutiérrez Alea and author/screenwriter Senel Paz have contended, I have to ask myself: in the process of arguing for this much needed tolerance in Cuba, why is it that the gay character is mocked, stereotyped, and ultimately sacrificed? As much in the story as in the film, the gay character is the one who seems preoccupied with sex, and therefore, the eroticism between two bodies portrayed in *Paradiso* is noticeably absent: "If you come home with me and you let me open your fly button by button, I'll lend [Vargas Llosa's novel] to you" (14), Diego says to David in the Coppelia ice cream parlor when they meet for the first time. On another occasion, Diego's discourse in the film projects a self-deprecating message: "I know that the goodness of fags is a double-edged sword."

At the start of this chapter, the official Cuban mind-set of the 1960s is discussed and documented as one that conveys the incompatibility of homosexuality and the Revolution. In these two texts that I am analyzing, this ideology is reinforced by the portrayal of homosexuals whose conduct is improper according to revolutionary doctrine. For example, Diego, the gay protagonist, gets hold of censored books, he does business in the black market with dollars, he has meetings with foreign diplomats, and he is an unfaithful friend. Another character, Germán, a gay sculptor, is silenced by the regime, and he sells himself in exchange for a trip off the Island. All of the previous characteristics catalogued under the revolutionary conscience as highly counterrevolutionary are part of the image of the gay that exudes from Gutiérrez Alea's film and Paz's short story, both from the early 1990s. On another level, and following the tradition of compulsory heterosexual narrative of the Western world, in these texts the gay characters are those who perform the duties of the *celestina* to resolve the erotic "problems" of the heterosexual characters. Despite the evident attraction and erotic-love desire that Diego has for David, the discourse of the former constantly represses that desire, a sacrifice that is complemented by Diego, who asks his friend Nancy to sleep with David in order to initiate him into heterosexual sexuality—"como debe ser" (as it should be). In a failed attempt to lessen the gap between these two erotic worlds, at the conclusion of the film, moments before Diego's departure, David, by Diego's request, hugs his gay friend after recounting the details of his first sexual encounter with Nancy. It is this minimal expression of affection with which the gay character must be satisfied. Diego's exile, represented similarly in *Fresa y chocolate* and in *El lobo, el bosque y el hombre nuevo,* as well as in Hernández Catá's 1928 novel mentioned earlier, fulfills the desire of heterosexual society in the sense that gays disappear, leaving ample room for the propagation of heterosexuality.

Writing on homosexual themes in Cuba during the last ten years, of course, is not limited to short stories and cinema. Without entering into a discussion of great detail, I could mention the poetry and drama of Abilio Estévez: *Manual de tentaciones* (1989), *La verdadera culpa de Juan Clemente Zenea* (1986) and *Juego con Gloria (*1986). This young writer presents the first case of openly homosexual poetry that has been published in Cuban journals.[24]

---

24. In a prose poem entitled "Mis tentaciones", Estévez writes "I would like to tell, to name all of my temptations, my very simple passions. There is no greater happiness than to lie oneself down to watch the lemon

Unlike Senel's short story, Estévez's poems contain verses in which the poet clearly acknowledges his homosexuality; that is, he expresses with a gender marker his attraction for a person of the same sex without having to make apologies.

In the field of music, it is important to note the song written and performed in concerts by singer-songwriter Pedro Luis Ferrer, "Amor de hombres," which serves as a precursor to the defense of gays who have been accused of being false revolutionaries and persecuted because of their sexual orientation: "they discriminate against him because he is that way/always waiting for someone similar/what fault is it of his if in his feelings/they put the weight of other morals ... so evident in his emotions," when in reality it is the opposite since "the kid turns out to be/an excellent worker ... and they don't rely on the others/when they call him to the guns/extra work and being on time." Ferrer takes another step on the contestatory ladder when he criticizes Cuban patriarchal heterosexuality that perseveres through the Revolution by denouncing "the little macho men who are used to treating their wives like slave drivers" and the official cupola of " the powerful ones that scandalize the neighborhood/by giving their children luxury cars." This song by Ferrer encourages a reconceptualization of the revolutionary individual that, from the outset, excluded homosexuals. In 1994, the famous troubadour Pablo Milanés, who incidentally, was one of the many young artists forced into the work camps of the UMAP in the 1970s, composed a song entitled "El pecado original" in which he presents "Two souls, two bodies,/two men who love each other" who "are going to be expelled/from the paradise in which they were made to live" and consequently he asks the audience to consider that "We are not God/let's not make another mistake."

---

shrub grow, and to wish for the rain, a rain without violence, falling over the beautiful body that dances for me, and a soft music—Vivaldi, Marcello, Frescobaldi—and a contralto voice" (63).

The long evolutionary process of homoerotic texts in Cuba is finally reclaiming its legitimate space in the Island's literature with the publication of works that will continue to be a source of inquiry and dialogue, and these works are not simply a "temporary fad" in the contemporary Cuban culture, as some have argued. Ultimately, the many years of official repression that negated, penalized, and ridiculed any cultural artistic expression that manifests a vision different from that of the institution have not been able to annihilate the human desire for the civil right to be different.

APPENDIX

ROUND TABLE WITH FOUR CUBAN INTELLECTUALS

CULTURE OF THE CUBAN REVOLUTION: A FLUCTUATING MOVEMENT

This interview was conducted in Havana on a hot afternoon in May, 1994. The four participants include poet, and at the time, director of Editorial Letras Cubanas, Juan Nicolás Padrón (presently associate editor of publications *of* Casa de las Américas); narrator and literary critic, Francisco López Sacha (currently, one of the vice presidents of the Artists and Writer's Union of Cuba, UNEAC); the director of *Revolución y cultura*, Elizabeth Díaz; and finally, musicologist, Silvana Padrón, Associate Editor of the music section of Editorial Letras Cubanas.

José B. Alvarez: I would like us to start this conversation from a theoretical point of view and discuss Marxism and Liberty, because I believe that Cuban culture, until 1968, still permitted certain possibilities towards the conceptualization of liberty within the Marxist ideology adopted in this country.

Juan Nicolás Padrón: Look, until '68, they weren't just discussing Marxism and Liberty, but also Existentialism and Liberty. You need to get *Lunes de revolución* to know what I'm talking about. Theater of the Absurd and Liberty, Marcusse (author of the book *The One-Dimensional Man* [1964]) and Liberty, Sartre (*What is Literature?*) and Liberty. That is to say, from '59 to '68, there were a series of ideological currents in Cuba, and I would also say that they were moving toward a type of liberty inside the cultural realm, like existentialism, socialism, and Marxism. *Lunes de revolución* was a space for that, but it wasn't the only one. Not too long ago, in *La gaceta de Cuba,* there was a controversy that revived the discussions of *Lunes de revolución.* Some people were affiliated with the group they defended, while others were a little more distanced from what they criticized. And others, of course, were saying between the lines that *Lunes de revolución* was a sectarian group. I believe that everyone has their own line of reasoning. Undeniably, the period between '59 and '68 had an extensive range of liberty, too extensive. I believe that it was almost a type of recklessness, because compared to what was being sent to the publishers, only the most marginal things were being published, and this doesn't happen in any country.

***Francisco López Sacha*:** Padrón, pardon me if I interrupt. What there was between '59 and '68 was fundamentally a period of diffusion. The "National Library Collection" ranged from Tomas Mann to Marcel Proust, from Joyce to Hemingway, to all authors. The Cuban cultural institutions were interested in diffusing the best of universal literature and the political-cultural and sociological thought of the twentieth century. The journals *RC,* now *Revolución y cultura,* as well as *Pensamiento crítico* (1966-70), started during this time. Included in this era were books on philosophy, published by the University of Havana, which also broached diverse and relevant features of national and universal culture. What was important was the diffusion. The new left had an influential role in this diffusion, because it was the moment in which the Cuban Revolution was doubting the traditional theoretical models and was making connections to Brecht, to Marcusse, to the new North American Left, to the New European Left, to the May Revolution, and to the strategies of Latin American guerrillas. What I mean is that all of these are different processes. Don't forget that it was a system politically linked to the Soviet Union, which taught us how to adapt ourselves to a revolutionary society.

J.N.P. In 1966, a little before 1968, they began to detect some contestatory symptoms in the publications, particularly in short story writing. In 1966, *Los años duros,* by Jesús Díaz, was published, and other novels and stories were emerging in which one began to see the presentation of the hero from a different perspective. So, at the beginning of 1966, this process was already being reverted to, and people were worried about a few of the publications which were printing rather scandalous things. Then, in 1968, *Los siete contra Tebas* and *Fuera de juego* appeared, two books which won awards in a competition sponsored by UNEAC. And listen to this; in the statement on the first page of both books, it says: "Our revolutionary condition permits us to point out that poetry and theater act as our enemies. The authors are the artists our enemies need to feed to the Trojan horse at the moment when imperialism decides to impose its warlike, face-to-face, political aggression against Cuba."

F.L.S. Listen, Padrón, you've got to take into account that 1966 was the crucial year of that decade for Cuban literature. Look what appeared in 1966: *Paradiso* by José Lezama Lima (1910-76); *Biografía de un cimarrón* by Miguel Barnet; *Los años duros* by Jesús Díaz; and *Pailock: el presditigitador* by Ezequiel Vieta. These are books that open four distinct paths in Cuban narrative. They established new paths in the life of Cuban literature. *Paradiso* for the novel, *Biografía de un cimarrón* for testimony, *Pailock* for fantasy writing, and *Los años duros* for short story writing. The four books are socio-political protests: *Paradiso* for all of the implications it contains; *Biografía* for the first appearance of a nude, and for the first narration of the experience of a runaway slave; *Los años duros* for the portrayal of that particular Cuban epic; and *Pailock* for the experience of imagination and of the absurd in the 1940s. What I'm saying is that all the lines of Cuban thought coming together here are those which emerge in works of universal maturity.

J.N.P. It is important to remember that we live in a political context where, in 1965, the government had created the Central Committee of the Communist Party of Cuba. On the political scene before 1965, they had first created the "Integrated Revolutionary Organizations" (ORI) and afterwards, the "United Party of the Socialist Revolution of Cuba" (PURSC), into which other organizations were also integrated. But up to 1965, there still wasn't a definition of the kind of militant political Marxism to which you are referring. It was only in '65 when the Central Committee of the Communist Party was created, that it was actually declared that a Marxist party was in power. I mean, one year later, important literature—as Sacha says—emerged. In fact, I think that in the case of *Paradiso*, a cycle is broken because one cannot forget that Lezama started with *Orígenes* (1944-56). The publication of that novel marked the end of a cycle. *Pailock* is something different; the problem with it is that it synthesizes the expression of the absurd, of fantasy, and of all of those elements which converge in the 1960s. Like Sacha said, the cases of *Los años duros* and *Biografía* effectively open up a completely new perspective. Barnet opens a perspective in the testimonial novel that later reemerges in testimony with *Girón en la memoria* (1970) by Victor Casaus (b. 1944); and *Conversación con el último norteamericano* (1973) by Enrique Cirules (b. 1938). In the end, this entire bibliography, which you already know about, was opened up by Barnet. And it was actually Jesús Díaz who opened the short story epoch, like that of the Golden Quinquennium (1966-70). The year 1968 was crucial because during it, apart from other international events that Sacha pointed out, there were the problems of the Czechoslovakian invasion, the troops of the Pact of Varsovia, and the massacre of Tlatelolco. What I mean is that there were a series of international events that happened one year after Che's death in Bolivia, that became the historical turning point in a sense. We all perceived a change in the national outlook. In 1968 there also was the Cultural Congress of Havana, the "Salón of Mai" and the Revolutionary Offensive (OR). These national events also marked the radicalization of the process of democratization that we had lived through in the period between '59 and '68. Of course, the expression of literature is no more than a reflection of all of this. I would say that it began to manifest itself as the opposition in this case. In opposition because *Fuera de juego* (1968) by Heberto Padilla, is not overtly oppositional, but rather, it can be depending on the way it is interpreted and the way I read it to you. But, yes, it is another type of opposition. However, you can figure that the UNEAC's jury's declaration for the poetry prize was signed by no less than José Talet, Manuel Díaz Martínez, José Lezama Lima, and César Calvo, among others, and it said, "The decision was unanimous. Cohen, who returning to his country, has left a written vote which coincides with the other four members of the jury." For them, there was no doubt. For them, *this* was the book.

J.B.A. Yes, but if you read the declaration of the theater jury, where the winner was *Los siete contra Tebas* (1968), by Antón Arrufat (b. 1935), you realize that the decision was three to two. Ricardo Salvat of Spain, Adolfo Gutkis of Argentina, and José Triana of Cuba all voted in favor. Those who voted against included Raquel Revuelta a Cuban, and Juan Larco a Peruvian. But if we put this in a Marxist context, leaving Leninism and Stalinism behind, I believe that we are confronting a period in which the best and most authentic expressions of Marxist Liberty are being published, even though you are defining it as libertine.

J.N.P. Let me explain why I understand it to be libertine. I believe that in that particular epoch, the people who managed the newspapers and journals were not conscious of their roles. I'm not talking about their roles as censors. I'm talking about the selection of works based on the best interests of the newspaper or journal, which exists in every part of the world. Really, if we are going to see censorship as an extreme case, we have to remember that there is censorship everywhere. You decide the material you use for your classes—you select. You don't publish freely, with carelessness or indecency. These people were not inclined to select in this way.

J.B.A. I agree with what you say in respect to censorship in the world, but here in Cuba there have been extreme cases which have been motivated strictly by politics. Let's look at the example of the articles of "Leopoldo Avila;" these were articles published in order to harm some specific intellectuals. That was official repression. Why did it happen?

F.L.S. You know, we are passing over a very important phenomenon that happened in the 70s, and that is the fight against the rebirth of socialist realism, and the way this fight was silenced by Che in *El hombre y el socialismo en Cuba* (1965). This is the book that put the limit on bureaucratic excesses, found fundamentally in the National Board of Culture. Che was the first to understand that it is not possible to create new literature without considering the cultural process of the nation. He also understood that popular tastes and preferences could not be determined by government functionaries, since ultimately, the people would not accept what the functionaries wanted. Che stopped the flood by attacking the rebirth of socialist realism in Cuba. This is a book from the year 1965—an important book because it defined the Revolution at that moment. Che says: "we have not suffered the errors of Eastern Europe, just the opposite, but we have the same problems to resolve. Above all, we have suffered an excess of censorship of our literature, cinema, fine arts," and what Che proposes is: "we are going to make art in another way. We are not going to 'implant' traditions; we are going to make sure future generations do not suffer the original sin like the non-revolutionary intellectuals of earlier years." This was the center of debate, and you can verify it with what was published in the journal *Casa de las Américas* during those years.

J.N.P. Let's go to your question; why does "Leopoldo Avila" surface? If you were to ask me this now, I would say, well, it seems to me that beginning in the 70s... Let's start with the economy to try to understand this. When they did away with the sugar quota, the siege began, and the blockade, the embargo, was put in place and Cuba had to look for other markets. It drew closer to the Soviet Union, who welcomed the Island. But Cuba had to accept the Soviet's economy, commerce, society, and the rest. You have to understand that a system cannot be isolated. Formulas began arriving on how to build a socialist society. I also remember a time when we defied the Russians by telling them that we were not trying to build just socialism—we were on the road to building socialism and communism at the same time; I'm talking about 1968. The revolutionary offensive was full of this spirit: "let's do away with all private property. The only things that should be private property are your toothbrush and your teeth." These were the terms and sentences of that epoch. Understandably, the politization reverted cultural politics; social and economic reverted to the culture of arts and letters. The reaction was to dictate norms and become the landlords of conduct, so that the revolutionary writers continued along this road. "Leopoldo Avila" appeared in this context.

Silvana Padrón: The death of Che in Bolivia, a very public fiasco, symbolized the loss of the Cuban model. Cuba was defending the possibility of a different model—a triumphant movement without the communists in front, one which would go against that of the Soviets and the Czechs. The death of Che signified the failure of all of the guerrilla fighters in Latin America because it produced the downfall of our resistance. We were left without a model, without the pretext we had been defending, and when you are left without a model...

J.B.A. So in this scene, Heberto Padilla appears. In this scene Anton Arrufat appears, along with "the short stories of violence"....

J.N.P. "The short stories of violence" were nothing more than a reflection. You've got to figure that at this time, what was seen in Cuba was the heroic literature from the Soviet Union. But what's happening is that we were having the "fight against bandits" in Cuba (in the Escambray mountains) and the heroic Soviet struggle that was reflected in the literature had a lot in common with the "fight against bandits." However, nothing is exactly alike, because the tropic is the tropic. What's more, we had traitors here, like they must have had there too, but their traitors are not reflected in the literature. So, what happened with the stories of violence? They drew an image of the hero that had nothing to do with that literature—with the classic literature of socialist realism—so people began to increasingly question the political leadership of the country. For example,"La vanguardia," by Norberto Fuentes, presents a protagonist that cheats on his own people, pretends to be with the Revolution but what he was doing was to make deals with the bandits. The vanguard, in this case, was the bandit. So we can talk about stories like that one or like "La caminata" by Heras León (which is found in *Los pasos en la hierba,* 1970). "La caminata" is about a fat man who is made to take a really long walk. This man can barely walk, but he is forced to finish. It's something inhumane. This type of literature reflects much of reality and reflects many human nuances, but it was criticized because it did not serve to unite us, to advance us on the "brilliant path." Again, I'll repeat that the laws of politics have nothing to do with aesthetics. Aesthetics reflect the reality of this moment. You are transcending reality in an aesthetic sense, but you have no reason to obey what might be politically expedient.

J.B.A. The antecedent to this is what you would see in the novel, *Mestra voluntaria* (1962), by Daura Olema García, when a group of youths climb Mount Turquino. Socialist realism tells you that at all cost you must praise the collective and individual sacrifices, in García's novel is the fact that the protagonists can go up and down Mount Turquino, and then go up it again if they chose. But in "La caminata", you see that the fat man can't do it, and that is something completely normal. This fits into the experience of any human being. Nevertheless, socialist realism says "yes," that one has to be able to because there can be no failure. This is what Heberto Padilla was rejecting.

J.N.P. Heberto also involved himself with another, more difficult problem. For this reason, I think that he was a writer of every epoch, because he has a poem entitled "En tiempos difíciles," that is a poem that speaks to our epoch as well. Listen to what he says:

> They asked that man for the time/ so that he would unite time with history/ They asked him for his hands/ because it was a difficult epoch/ nothing is better than a pair of good hands./ They asked him for his eyes/ that sometimes shed tears/ to contemplate the bright side/ (especially the bright side of life)/ because the horror is enough for one frightened eye./ They asked him for his lips/ dried out and cracked in order to assure,/ to create, with each statement, a dream (the best dream);/ they asked for his legs/ hard and knotted,/ (his old walking legs)/ because in difficult times/ is there anything better than construction and the trench?/ They asked him for the forest he had nourished since his childhood,/ with his faithful tree./ They asked him for his chest, his heart, his shoulders./ They said/ that it was highly necessary./ They explained to him afterwards/ that everything had been a useless donation/ without giving them his tongue/ because without giving them his tongue/ [and this relates to the analysis that I have been doing]/ because in difficult times/ nothing is as useful to stop hate as the lie./ And finally, they begged him/ that, please, go out for a walk/ because in difficult times/ this is, without a doubt, the decisive test.

J.B.A. This poem contains everything that you could want. It is as apropos now as it was 30 years ago, and that is the nature of art. But in '68...

J.N.P. Now it's curious that around these years they were presenting poems that would later be vindicated. One example is a poem by Raul Rivero (b. 1945). This poem was published many years later, but it was full of this spirit. Think about it, so that you understand the turns of history. I'm first going to read you one of Rivero's poems, and then I'm going to recite another one from memory because it's not published and is the opposite of the first one - you, who are looking for explanations for why someone would write one thing after writing something else. Raul Rivero wrote a poem called "Panfleto" (*Papel de hombre*, 1970). Listen to it:

> He who proposes to find in these verses words which speak to the critics, that voice saved by the pure poets in the hurricane of 1959 needs not to continue. Stop reading right now, stop on this very line. Because here my companions of Battalion 12 appear, be surprised to find out that they died and also fought for culture in the mountains of Escambray. Here, Conrado Benítez and Manuel Ascuza will be spoken of, of their quick deaths like mountain rivers. Adjectives will be used and they will say in this poem that the martyrs died heroically, that the peasant farmers gained their historic power, that the workers fought like lions and like stubborn workers with guns. This poem will be understood. Be careful that you don't get too close to the critics with their critical judgements of this poem because the union assembly is now here. And in these types of meetings they almost never speak about troublesome things. They almost never speak of lewd, metaphysical sensations [...] Here the bandits are interrogated, there are 'damn', 'whore,' 'of your mother', yells, from hell, they killed me. Hours and hours of lookout and vigil. There are children in combat, murdered women, destroyed houses, as if there were no ivory towers. But there is no rhyme, there are no possibilities to study the cadence and the hemstitch. This is a pamphlet. There is no music, it lacks inner rhythm, what you hear are the evils they put here during the middle century. Those who are passing are blacks with drums asking Fidel, Fidel, what does Fidel have? That which passes is a man reading the *La carretera de Bocolans*, those which pass are dead, that only yesterday arrived with the portraits of their girlfriends in their wallets, with the first beard without shaving, and now they will stay in a school, in a cooperative. Don't look for influences, they are not in the reports, in the publishing houses, the experiences and the conversations. This is a pamphlet [...] What will the Jorge Luis Borges' say about this? But above all, who cares what Jorge Luis Borges says of this. Here we have only a man working the land, and another teaching a child, and yet another

cutting cane, and there is another one in front of a machine that bottles pineapple jelly. There is no poetry in so much daily life. The critics need not to continue reading now because there is a central meeting of the Party; the professors need not to look with their academic eyes because what we have here is a man being self-critical.

This poem isn't saying anything transcendental, but think about what's happening. In the early 1980s, almost at the height of that process, Raúl Rivero read a poem in Camagüey that began by saying: "I wrote this poem alone, without the generous and selfless help of the Soviet Union," and then began to say something like: "Our ministers..." (When I began to listen to Raul Rivero reciting this poem, I thought that it was the same pamphlet that he had read to me years before), "Our ministers do not have Swiss Bank accounts / our ministers do not have yachts or houses / our ministers are not going fishing every Sunday / our ministers have nothing except their ministries," and so on. Do you know what is the final verse that disqualifies everything before it? It say: "They are not in need of any of that." Do you understand? This is the same man who writes one thing and then another one that refutes himself. This began in 1968, when the short stories of violence began and when they began to reject the hero. No, not to reject him, but to (re)create him, to say what the Cuban hero is really like—the same one that they kill in the "fight against bandits," is the same one that does other things. With this new criterion began a new stage for literature and for Cuban culture. What's more, if you analyze the first book by Chino Heras, *La guerra tuvo seis nombres* (1968), you see that there are six stories and each one has its title a personal name and the text that follows is the story of that individual. When you begin with the short stories of Chino in that first book and then end up with *Los pasos en la hierba* (1970) where you find "La caminata"—a short story that I have already talked about—and "La noche del capitán"—whose protagonist is a cowardly captain—you begin to realize that there is a new political and social process in a period of four or five years and that its crude reality is reflected in literature.

S. P. But in that epoch, reality was reflected in everything—in the music too. Silvio Rodríguez has a song titled: "Playa Girón" that says, "If someone steals my food and then gives his life, what can be done?" This conflict that you talk about is seen in everything and everywhere.

J.N.P. In the Golden Quinquennium there are short stories that, perhaps, have not been outstanding. However, *Escambray 60* (1970) by Hugo Chinea (b. 1939), and *Usted sí puede tener un Buick* (1969) by Sergio Chaple (b. 1938) are important books. There are classic books too, which support the thesis of the Golden Quinquennium. There is a richness reflected in the literature of this period. I'm talking about a phase that began in 1968 and ended, I would say, in 1976. It is a time in which everything is reoriented, when the 10 Million Ton Harvest (1970) begins, which was the most important event to happen in Cuba during this epoch, because after the failure of the harvest, economic strategy in Cuba was redirected.

F.L.S. I have a book which is in the process of being published, and it includes my essays about the Cuban short story between 1966 and 1972, which was the time of this literary explosion, the world. At this time, three very clear tendencies emerged: 1)"Violence" where we find Jesús Díaz (*Los años duros* [1966], *Las iniciales de la tierra* [1987], *Las palabras perdidas* [1992]); Chino Heras (*La guerra tuvo seis nombres* [1968], *Los pasos en la hierba* [1970], *Acero* [1977], *A fuego limpio* [1980]); Norberto Fuentes (*Condenados de condado* [1968], *Hemingway en Cuba* [1988]), and others. 2)"Change": a tendency to argue that one is "seeing the past with contemporary eyes." Its best representatives are Manuel Cofiño (b. 1936; *Tiempo de cambio* [1969], *La última mujer y el próximo combate* [1971], *Cuando la sangre se parece al fuego* [1977], *Amor a sombra y sol* [1980], *Andando por ahí, por esas calles* [1982]); Sergio Chaple (*Hacia otra luz más pura* [1975]); Hugo Chinea and others. 3)Finally, "fable-like", which follows a Cuban tradition and is embodied best by Antonio Benítez Rojo (b. 1931); (*El escudo de hojas secas* [1969], *El mar de las lentejas* [1979], *Tute de reyes* [1967]). Now, that lasts until 1972. These are tendencies that, in certain ways, regard both past and present in Cuba, but in the period between 1972 and 1976 these trends die. Violence is schematized by other authors. The change is imposed as a norm of study and the fable perishes, remaining only very tenuously in books by Miguel Collazo (b. 1936; *El libro fantástico de Oaj* [1966], *El laurel del patio grande* [1978], and *Onoloria* [1973]). It was a period that privileged the notion that art was, above all, ideology, and that was, in my opinion, the fundamental error of the Gray Quinqennium, or if you like, the "Black Decennium." The right to subordinate art to ideology was the central error of Cuban cultural politics from 1971 until 1977 or 1978, and that is what guided Cuban political culture. What's more, it was a period in which Cuba had its best commercial and economic relations with Russia. Cuba entered CAME, and it believed, as I say in the novel I'm currently writing, that capitalism was bullshit, and that it was going to end. Then they began to reformulate literature in a distinct way. They began to see art as a special manifestation of the human conscience, and not necessarily subordinated to a particular ideology dictated by politics. The struggle of this generation was to separate art from its previous role as a permanent manifestation of ideology.

J.N.P. The climatic moment of this period was the year 1971. You really have to appreciate two sub-phases inside the period 1968-1976. The first phase lasted until 1971, which was a time of great conflicts. These were the years of the Golden Quinquennium for the short story, the time of the Padilla case in poetry, and Arrufat in theater and the consequences that that left. For example, I can tell you that theater was over. I would say that the genre most affected by all of these problems was the theater. Not even the short story or the novel, it was the theater. When you analyze the quantity of plays that were produced here from 1959-1968 and those produced between 1968-1971, you see that one period is very different from the other. It's as if they came from two different countries. Here, *La noche de los asesinos* (1965) by Jose Triana; Dos viejos pánicos (1968) by Virgilio Piñera (1912-79; *La carne de René* [1952], *Aire frío* [1959], *El parque de la fraternidad* [1962], *Pequeñas maniobras* [1963], *La muerte del ñeque* [1964]). It is incredible to think of the first rate plays that Héctor Quintero (b. 1942) wrote during those years, *(El premio flaco* [1966], *Teatro* [1978], *Diez cuentos teatralizados* [1985]). Also, Abelardo Estorino (b. 1925; *El robo del chochino* [1964]) was very productive. Suddenly, all of this was gone. They were held back and silenced.

S.P. You must also consider the attacks against homosexuals during those years.

J.N.P. The repression of the homosexuals was a revolutionary attack, the majority of the homosexuals were right there, in theater. Either they continued to write in silence or they did not write any longer. I believe that 1971 was the ultimate manifestation of this type of politics. The National Congress of Education and Culture was the consummation of Sovietization in Cuban culture; the official declaration stated that it was going to be socialist realism or nothing. It seems to me that this was the most extreme moment of this painful process and that it left many consequences. Of course, in 1971, the Gray Quinquennium began in narrative, and in theater the repression lasted until they tried to revive the Escambray Theater in the 1970s.

F.L.S. No, Escambray Theater emerged earlier, in 1968, or rather, the Escambray that rescued us from this crisis. It was due to their willingness to go up to the mountains of Escambray and to distinguish their theater from that of Havana—or to do theater from positions other than purely aesthetic. There were theater seminars given for the people of the Escambray ensemble to show them that the theater they were doing was not entirely consistent with the Revolution and that they had left studio theater to work in Escambray. But this was a personal choice, not a directive.

J.N.P. I'm going to point out something very interesting to you. I don't know as much about theater as Sacha, but in that era, they rejected studio theater in order to do theater in the natural environment, in open spaces with the people. But now, when you go to the National Institute of Art (ISA), you find groups doing Shakespeare. They rejected Shakespeare and now they have gone back to him, figure that.

F.L.S. There is one interesting fact. Yes, the theater had personal participation; it was not marked by the beginning of the Gray Quinquennium and I'm going to tell you why. Until the year 1970-71, Escambray Theater worked as an individual, organic group, and afterwards became a model, especially after 1972. After Fidel saw the presentation of *La vitrina* in Escambray, it was taken to be the model of theater that all were expected to imitate. It was not because Escambray wanted this, but because the government said so, and that in some way, Escambray's method became the model for Cuban theater, a good model. It was also considered a model in Colombia and other countries. What happened is that after this, certain groups began to imitate Escambray and a false dichotomy—or a division—was created between studio theater and theater done in the mountains or on the street. This dichotomy hurt Cuban theater in the long run, because it was said that studio theater was old and that theater for the people was new. This was false. Yes, it was a different type of theater. Then the Ministry of Culture itself privileged theater done in the mountains and in the cities in the interior (away from Havana). This created a dispute which began in the Congress of Education and Culture and lasted until 1980 when the two groups united since their goals and the final results were the same; symbolically, Raquel Revuelta and Sergio Corrieri embraced each other at the Theater Festival of Havana in 1980. That was when the line between studio theater and "New Theater" was erased; from then on, there was one single theater, done either in Escambray or in Havana. So, from this point on, there was a different understanding confronting the theater, but it's important to note that it wasn't the fault of Escambray. Escambray was an authentic occurrence in Cuban theater—it was not something fabricated. In contrast, other small groups did fabricate something in the image and likeness of Escambray. Escambray knew that they were doing Cuban theater, just as Teatro Estudio was doing, as well as other groups in Havana. Now, 1980 signifies the comeback of Vicente Revuelta, Roberto Blanco, Pepe Santos, and a number of other Cuban artists that had been marginalized in the 1970s, accused of homosexuality. They returned to Cuban theater with plays, with groups, with unique dispositions, and created heterogeneity in national theater; this was after 1980, which was a key year in Cuban theater. It was when Cuban theater was united through its diversity, and it was also when Cuban artists were recognized as part of just one theater, not a theater for an audience of farmers or for an urban public, but just one single theater. This conscience was what allowed Cuban theater of the 1980s to progress so rapidly, progressing at a rhythm which has continued to accelerate up to the present day.

J.B.A. Let's back up to 1968 to examine what was happening between that year, when the polemic books of Antón Arrufat and Heberto Padilla were published, and the year 1971, when *Los pasos en la hierba* by Heras León was published. What was written and why?

F.L.S. There is a transition. Look, in 1970, *La cantidad hechizada* by Lezama Lima was published...

J.N.P. I'm going to tell you something that, for sure, Sacha will not agree with. There are two loops. The Gray Quinquennium was not so gray and the Golden Quinquennium was not so golden, as with everything, because both were open periods. If you review some of the publications from the Gray Years, you see that there are some great titles. In this period they published works of Alejo Carpentier, *Pan dormindo* (1975) by José Soler Puig, *Aventuras de Guille* (1975), *El cochero azul* (1975), *Gente de mar* (1977) by Dora Alonso (b. 1910); and, a book by Onelio Jorge Cardoso (b. 1914), *El hilo y la cuerda* (1975); however, all of these people were outside of that first loop. This is the first time I have said this because until now I did not have the elements of judgement that my recent research has provided me, which backs up my argument that there were two loops, one closed and the other open.

F.L.S. Open for whom?... For those who had a name and had been tried for loyalty in the process?

J.N.P. In addition to loyalty, they had proven their rank as good writers which made them "untouchables." I can tell you more; there were also lesser known writers like Julio Travieso (b. 1940; *Días de guerra* [1967], *Los corderos beben vino* [1970], *Para matar al lobo* [1971], *Cuando la noche muera* [1983]); Noel Navaro (b. 1931; *Los días de nuestra angustia* [1962], *Los caminos de la noche* [1967], *La huella del pulgar* [1972], *Donde cae la luna* [1977], *El nivel de la aguas* [1980]); and Gustavo Erugen, (*Los lagartos no comen queso*). All these that I have mentioned, as well as a few others, published good literature in those years.

F.L.S. Yes, but in spite of these loops, there was a generally repressive climate that dominated the agenda, and that was very difficult to overcome.

J.B.A. So, from 1968 to 1971 there was no political protest that looked critically at the situation in the country?

J.N.P. I believe that the Padilla case and the Arrufat case paralyzed that. Certain novels emerged in 1970 or 1971, like *Saccharío* (1970) by Miguel Cosio (b. 1938), and *La última mujer y el próximo combate* (1971) by Manuel Cofino (b. 1938), which initiated a new type of novel. Not too long ago, I was reviewing essays written from 1971 to 76, and—although I'm introducing another genre it's relevant—I came to realize that all writers in this epoch were dedicating their efforts to writing about the past, or to Latin America. Everyone started talking about José María Heredia (1803-39), Julián del Casal (1863-93), and Sor Juana Inés de la Cruz (1651-95); you see, everyone turned to the past and nobody was writing essays about what was actually happening in Cuba.

F.L.S. There was also a mandate originating at the National Congress of Culture that stipulated that Cuban roots had to be rescued.

J.N.P. That has something to do with *estodoncismo* and *negrometrajes* (the representation of Cuban blacks in film). *Estodoncismo* was a trend during this time period... What Sacha was telling you is true, but it also resulted in a series of manifestations or tendencies. For example, the trend in poetry was to rescue the roots through the *sin son*, birds, nature, and trees, a sort of rudimentary ecology. So the tendency of the *negrometrajes* was to make all their films refer to the blacks, the past, slavery. Everyone turned to the past. I'm not disqualifying the term, Gray Quinqennium, but I am enriching it with more complicated things...

F.L.S. Much more was lost in 1976. What happened was that Rafael Soler (1945-75) appeared in the arena of the Cuban short story, with *Campamento de artillería, Un hombre en la fosa* and *Noche de fósforos*. Its view was a little less prejudiced, but not particularly original. It was the adolescent's perspective of the Revolution and not that of the adult, and this was innovative. Also the novel *Comandante veneno*, by Manuel Pereira (b. 1948), was published and he also presented an adolescent protagonist who looked to the past, or to the beginning of the Revolution, and that was new. This change resulted in a generational tendency to reflect Cuban youth in the first years of the Revolution, beginning with Miguel Mejides (b. 1950) and with Senel Paz (b. 1950; *Un rey en el jardín* [1983], *El lobo, el bosque y el hombre nuevo* [1991], "Las hermanas" [1993]) and continued into the 1980s, with myself, with Abel Prieto (b. 1950; *No me falles, Gallego* [1983]), with Arturo Arango, and with Reinaldo Montero. On a certain level it critique the systematization, but it was just the beginning and it was the way to explore a series of problems that were not being addressed. But it was still looking at conflict, in this case the dialectic of Man-History. From my perspective, in the 1960s literature examined History and Man, but beginning in the late 1970s, Man was placed first and History was second, but always under the same closed loop.

J.N.P. I would have to add that, beginning in the 80s, we begin to see man and his histories; the recount of a single history was over...

F.L.S. As a result, a very tangible style emerged in 1987. This year was a turning point for the Cuban short story because it was the moment in which our generation of writers matured and at the same time a new generation of writers was born. I distinguish between a "generation" and a "promotion." We were the second promotion of the generation of *El caimán barbudo* (1966-85, 96-present), those born between 1940 and 1955. The following generation arrived with a different air about them. They had the advantage that they did not have any traumatic ruptures in their generational development within Cuban politics.

J.N.P. What I'm telling you is that starting in 1976, there was a process, like I've already described, which had a moment of rupture in 1980. The year 1980 was very crucial. Jimmy Carter was the only American president that had gotten close to Cuba; under his presidency, the American Interests Section came into being, and the so called "Cuban Community" began to travel to Cuba, but all this ended in 1980. During that time I was a professor; when everything began to happen in 1980, I remember well that the students were telling me that they wanted to get into the embassy because "everything they've told us has been a lie. They don't chase black people with dogs in the United States." So, the strategies of the 40s and 50s were being repeated in Cuban education in the 80s, and therefore, the students thought that the persecution of the blacks was the same as in the earlier decades, and that was a myth. I could give you 15-20 myths about the United States promoted here: workers are dying of hunger, the living conditions of the workers are awful, etc. All of these myths or clichés had been assimilated by the youth, because it is much easier to tell these things to them. What happens is that when young people from the Cuban community in the United States began arriving, another truth was revealed. I would have liked to have shown you the poem by Osvaldo Sánchez, because the first rupture that I felt in literature occurred with this poem in 1981. It's called *Matar el último venado*. Look at this book and you will see how this disillusionment is reflected. It may be reflected in a way that you can barely recognize, but it was a rupture. This new generation began to doubt everything that they were told, they began to question things, they began to act as people who scrutinized reality, they began to penetrate this reality. All of this was the unchaining of the 80s.

F.L.S. Furthermore, in an article titled "Jesús Díaz y la inter-Rogación" published in the journal *Casa de las Américas*, 182, I talk about the aesthetic of interrogation; that is, how we began to interrogate Cuban social processes. A large amount of short stories and novels that appeared during this period focused on the interrogation of the 60s, 70s, and 80s. The current process of rupture is very different from what ours was; we departed from the ethical level because our concern was to reflect on the ethical problems of our day. On the other hand, the current generation takes the ethical as secondary; theirs is more so a level of existential anguish or an escape from a few minutes of reality. It's not a divorce from reality, but rather a focus on unpublished perspectives of reality. In the 1980s, we did not explore these perspectives, but we are now as we keep publishing like previous generations of writers. I know that you are amazed to find out that Lisandro Otero (b. 1932; *La situación* [1963], *La pasión de Urbino* [1966],

General a caballo [1980], *Temporada de ángeles* [1983], *Arbol de la vida* [1990]) has written about certain contemporary themes that are controversial. Lisandro's writing comes from processes in which there are answers to Cuban social problems. People forget—and I have said many times—that Lisandro Otero won the National Journalism Award in 1953 with a report about the Algerian guerrillas and that he risked his own life writing that report. It doesn't surprise me that Lisandro's first book on the Revolution would have been *Cuba, Z.D.A.*, in 1960, and it doesn't surprise me that one of Lisandro's most important books would be *Razón y fuerza de Chile*, published in 1974. Lisandro has always been a journalist. What amazes me is not that Lisandro does journalism, but rather that he could say some things that we assume he would have known since the 80s, but that chose not to write about them in the 80s. That is what worries me.

J.B.A. What happens between 1976 and 1980?

F.L.S. There isn't anything in particular, but there is a change. The change is toward a narrative that explores children's and adolescent's experiences in the Revolution.

J.B.A. Yes, Senel Paz, Rafael Soler, Sánchez Mejides, who write about the "becarios," their experiences in Havana, their participation in the Revolution, etc. So, what happens from 1980 to 1987?

F.L.S. Fundamentally, it is a change in perspective; the conflict is not longer one of history toward the individual, but of the individual toward history. The "I." First let's observe the individual and then we see what happens to this individual within history.

J.B.A. Who introduced this "I"?

F.L.S. Everyone. Mejides and Senel introduced it first, and then Arturo Arango, Abel Prieto, Reinaldo Montero, myself and others, followed. Look, Pepe, the change really began in the 1960s with the stories of Jesús Díaz, like "Amor a la patria," or "Parque de diversiones," but it was interrupted in 1972. The change really began at the end of the 60s, but it was stopped very quickly...

J.B.A. So in reality, it wasn't a change. It was actually a continuation of...

F.L.S. Exactly. It was a natural consequence in a process of authenticity.

J.B.A. What came afterwards, indeed was a change, a rupture...

F.L.S. Of course. This point of view already existed in Chino Heras and even in Cofiño, and in Jesús Díaz, but it stopped until it emerged again in Rafael Soler, in Senel Paz, and in the narrators I mentioned earlier.

J.B.A. In those years, the self-censorship of the past didn't exist anymore.

F.L.S. I don't think so, at least not in my generation, but one would have to question a few other writers. I never felt it.

J.B.A. I haven't read all of your narrative work, but, in your story "Dorado mundo" (Short Story Award from la Gaceta de Cuba, 1992), I see—from the point of view of someone who has not lived the Cuban reality—a reinterpretation of history. Before "Dorado mundo," what did you write that presented this revision of history?

F.L.S. I have a book called *Descubrimiento del azul*, from 1987, where I have already presented this point of view, and where I question man's role in society. It is a meeting between Emilio Zola and Augusto Strindberg in the French comedy, the night of December 18, 1879. Also, the same year *Don juanes* by Reinaldo Montero; *Forastero*, by Luis Manuel García; *Se permuta esta casa* by Guillermo Vidal; and, *We All Live in a Yellow Submarine* and

Descubrimiento del azul, which were mine, were published in Cuba. These books were fragmenting "history" and rewriting it in a different way. This phenomenon includes short stories by Ricardo Ortega, Senel Paz, and Luis Manuel García. There was a turning point when, for the first time, Cuban narrative broke away from the single theme Cuban story and did away with chronologies. I did it in 1987, and in that same year, the new generation appeared: Sánchez Mejides, Roberto Urías, Amil Valle, Rogelio Saunders, and Alberto Garrido (who was, for me, the best of them). That is, one cycle ended and another generation appeared, which, to a certain degree, negated us. They began to discuss contemporary Cuban problems in a distinct way. What happened? In that era, writers of that new generation were divided into distinct categories: "The Violent" (*Los Violentos*) and "The Exquisite" (*Los Exquisitos*). "The Violent" include the writers that I just mentioned. They were called this because they were dead set on breaking the traditional narrative thread in their stories. Then "The Exquisite" appeared, and they began to experiment. They said that it was not experimentation, that is was a normal way of writing, but everything began to break down—it was an evident rupture with everything that had been done up to that moment. They began to experiment with the form and began to create stories which were fragments, pieces. They began to mix genres, and also began to create characters, who were—as Antonio Ponte point out—larvae, worms, characters who aren't human.... They were creating a characters that you could not imagine. So, they started to treat history in a different way. Furthermore, they began to divide The Violent and The Exquisite. Sacha already had a great theory about this experimentation of the Cuban story through the 80s. He argues that there wasn't just The Exquisite and The Violent, but also The Freaks (*Los Freakies*) and The Rockers (*Los Roqueros*).

Listen, I have just turned an essay in to Elizabeth Díaz which discusses four groups existing today: the rockers, the iconoclasts, the traditionalists, and the fablemakers. The conception of the rockers, is that of the young people who are breaking new ground; the conception of the traditionalist is that they were the people that had some level of respect for the traditional organization of the story. The iconoclasts, who included Sánchez Mejides and others, did not respect any of it; and the fablemakers began with the nucleus of Moterroso, Cortázar, and above all, Borges; this is the other trend that appeared in 1994, this very year. This is where, we would say, another generation of short story writers begins. The first novel of this group, to a certain degree, is *Matariles*, by Guillermo Vidal...

J.N.P. An excellent novel that you have to read. It's a typical protest novel. I'm talking about something straight out of the oven.

F.L.S. ... and *Sangre azul* by Zoé Valdés (b. 1959; *Todo para una sombra* [1986], *La nada cotidiana* [1995], *Te di la vida entera* [1996], *Traficantes de belleza* [1998]), but for me, the most contestatory novel in the 90s is *Martariles*.

***Elizabeth Diáz*:** The other day I heard someone talking about a novel by one of the *Novísimos*—Pablo Aguiar—that sounded incredible. He read a crazy fragment and it was about four guys in a clandestine brewery. What a crazy novel!

J.N.P. It's a shame that you are not able to get that book. I can't give it to you because it's the only one I have... There's another group of writers in narrative and poetry that I would say is lead by Alberto Rodríguez Torres, and it is of philosophical reflection.

F.L.S. The tradition initiated by Raúl Hernández Novás...

J.N.P. Exactly. It goes back to interrogating a series of human problems, problems of men and general problems that transcend history; these writers are lead by Alberto Rodríguez Torres. He has a book of poetry called *Todas las jaurías del rey* (1987), that is a key book since it inaugurates this line. In the short story, he is followed by Raúl Aguiar and Jorge Luis Arzola. Arzola is a very young writer and has a small book of stories called *Prisioneros del círculo de horizonte*, that is very good and addresses things that have happened to him; it is autobiographical. There is another book that is very important, that hasn't had any followers yet, since it's so new, but it will have. It is a book by Angel Santiesteban called *Sur: latitud 13*, that won a honorary mention in the Casa de las Américas competition. It's a book with various stories, (including one which has the same title as the book), that reflect on the themes of the war in Angola and of internationalism, but through a new perspective, one that is not the official vision. I say the official vision not because it is officially stated, but because traditionally, when one refers to the war in Angola, to internationalism, he almost always does so in a compact form, unanimous, definite. However, *in Sur: latitud 13,* there is one individual who has his conflict. It revitalizes and segments the problem of the violence addressed by the writers in the 1960s, but framed within the new context of internationalism.

S.P. Remember that Angel is a student of Chino Heras.

F.L.S. Of course, and he is one of those that I now call a traditionalist...

J.N.P. In his writings the "violent" short story continues, and we can talk about a tradition. "Sur: latitud 13" is about a Cuban violinist who is in the army deployed in Angola and who always has his violin with him. It's really pretty interesting. He is presenting a standard by which people can feel good. In the evolution of the events, his fellow soldiers reject him and say that they don't need the violin and demand that he gives up his violin; he is obligated to exchange it for food and medicine. It is a song, a cry, for the necessity of art in the most difficult moments.

J.B.A. Alberto Garrido and Alejandro Alvarez have also recreated that sort of violence in *Cañón de retrocarga*. Last time we talked you told me that Garrido was writing a novel called *Café irlandés*. What is happening with that project?

J.N.P. He has not finish it. It is taking him too long.

J.B.A. You told me that the book addressed a theme from three points of view: a homosexual, a hippie, and a brilliant university student.

J.N.P. You remember everything that I've told you before....

F.L.S. My friend, Padrón, when someone eats steak and writes it down, you can never forget it...

J.B.A. To clarify things, I don't eat meat in the United States...

F.L.S. I stand corrected. When someone eats vegetables and writes it down, you can never forget it. But since here in Cuba we don't eat either steak or vegetables...

J.B.A. Let's get back to *Café irlandés*. I have never read any part of the text, but the idea of the three points of view seems very suggestive to me...

J.N.P. He once read me part of the text, but I never saw it again. I think that it could be an interesting novel because it really breaks up certain myths. *Cañón de retrocarga* still hasn't been published.

J.B.A. A fragment of it was published in number 17 or 18 of the journal *Letras cubanas*.

F.L.S. This guy is really well informed! Wow. Down to the last detail!

J.N.P. Let me tell you something, Pepe, of those people living outside of Cuba, you have been one of the most informed about Cuban literature, and I have visited thousands of people. Do you know a story by Ricardo Arrieta called "La horma"? I think it is a very important story for your theme.

F.L.S. And also various short stories in number 19 of *Letras cubanas*, especially "La culpa" by Ricardo Arrieta.

J.B.A. It seems like *Letras cubanas* has been the vanguard of everything that has interested me for years. Also, *La gaceta de Cuba*, starting with your short story, Sacha, is following in the steps that *Letras cubanas* initiated in their number 9 issue. Let's hope that the trend continues.

WORKS CITED

Alcalá, Rosa María. "Algunas reflexiones en torno al cuento."*Escritos* 7 (1991): 7-14.

Almendros, Néstor y Orlando Jiménez Leal. Dirs. *Conducta impropia*. 1984.

Altamiranda, Daniel. "Lezama Lima, José." *Latin American Writers on Gay and Lesbian Themes: A Bio-Critical Sourcebook.* Ed. David William Foster. Westport, Conn.: Greenwood Press, 1994. 202-11.

Alvarez IV, José Bernardo. "Literatura cubana de los 80: una visión sin censura." *Torre de papel* 3 (1993): 85-98.

———. "Ruptura en la narrativa social cubana: Novísimos y Novísimas." *Torre de papel* 5.1 (1995): 61-75.

———. "Desarrollo de la narrativa cubana de las últimas décadas: el Quinquenio Gris y sus consecuencias." *Mester* 23.2 (1994): 129-56.

Alzandúa, Gloria. "To(o) Queer the Writer—Loca, escritora y chicana." *InVersions: Writings by Dykes, Queers and Lesbians.* Ed. Betsy Warland. Vancouver: Press Gang Publishers, 1991. 249-63.

Arenas, Reinaldo. *Antes que anochezca.* México, D.F.: Tusquets Editores, 1992.

Arguelles, Lourdes y B. Ruby Rich. "Homosexuality, Homophobia, and Revolution: Notes Toward an Understanding of the Cuban Lesbian and Gay Male Experience, Part I." *Signs* 9.4 (1984): 683-99.

Atkinson, Grace. "Radical Feminism." *Notes from the Second Year.* Ed. Shulamith Firestone y Anne Koedt. New York: Morrow, 1970.

Avila, Leopoldo. "Las provocaciones de Padilla." *Verde olivo* 10 nov. (1968): 17-18.

———. "Sobre algunas corrientes de la crítica y la literatura cubana." *Verde olivo* 24 nov. 1968: 14-18.

Baquero, Gastón. "Dulce M. Loynaz, la política y el exilio." *Nuevo Herald* [Miami, Fla] 14 de abril 1993: 14A.

Bardach, Ann Louise. "Fidel Castro, a los 67 años: 'debemos peocuparnos más por el destino de las ideas que por el destino de los hombres'." *Proceso internacional* 919 (1994): 50-51.
Barnet, Miguel. Entrevista teléfonica. 22 de mayo de 1993.
Benítez Rojo, Antonio. *La isla que se repite.* Hanover, NH: Ediciones del Norte, 1989.
Benjamin, Medea. "Things Fall Apart." *NACLA* 24.2 (1990): 13-22.
Bianchi Ross, Ciro. "Como las cartas no llegan: correspondencia trunca, olvidada o perdida que descubre preocupaciones, odios y amores del autor de *Paradiso*." *La gaceta de Cuba* 3 (1994): 15-20.
Bunck, Julie Marie. *Fidel Castro and the Quest for a Revolutionary Culture in Cuba.* University Park: Pennsylvania State U P, 1994.
Cabrera Infante, Guillermo. Prefacio. *Así en la paz como en la guerra.* Barcelona: Seix Barral, 1971. 7-11.
Carreño, Enrique. "Macaos." *Letras cubanas* 14 (1990): 174.
Castro, Fidel. "Discurso pronunciado en la clausura del segundo congreso de la FMC." *Boletín de la FMC* (s.f, s.p).
Childers, Joseph y Gary Hentzy, eds. *Columbia Dictionary of Modern Literary and Cultural Criticism.* New York: Columbia U P, 1994.
Comité Director de la UNEAC. "Declaración de la UNEAC." Los siete contra Tebas. Antón Arrufat. La Habana: Ediciones Unión, 1968. 7-16.
Cortázar, Julio. "Algunos aspectos del cuento." *Casa de las Américas* 15-16 (1962-63): 3-14.
_____. "Del cuento breve y sus alrededores." *Ultimo round.* México: Siglo Veintiuno, 1970.
_____. *Vuelta al día en ochenta mundos.* México, D.F.: Siglo Veintiuno Editores, 1969.
De Bruyn, Frans. "Eagleton, Terry." *Encyclopedia of Contemporary Literary Criticism.* Ed. Irena Makaryk. Toronto: U of Toronto P, 1993. 301-03.
De Man, Paul. *Blindness and Insight: Essays in the Rhetoric of Contemporary Criticism.* 2nd ed. Minneapolis: U of Minnesota P, 1983.
"Declaración del Primer Congreso Nacional de Educación y Cultura." *Unión* 1-2 (1971): 6-13.
"Declarations of the First National Congress of Education and Culture." *Granma Weekly Review* [La Habana] 9 de mayo de 1971: 5.
Del Río, Joel. "Una declaración de amor." *Revolución y cultura* 1 (1995): 34.

Di Tella, Torcuato, Gajardo Paz, Susana Gamba y Hugo Chumbita, eds. *Diccionario de ciencias sociales y políticas*. Buenos Aires: Puntosur Editores, 1989.

Díaz Méndez, Alberto. "El turismo yanqui en América Latina." *El caimán barbudo* 61 (1972): 10-11.

Díaz, Jesús. *Los años duros*. Buenos Aires: Editorial Jorge Alvarez, 1967.

Dirección Política de las FAR. Prólogo. *Tiempo de cambio*. Manuel Cofiño. La Habana: Dirección Política de las FAR, 1969.

Dufrenne, Michael. *In the Presence of the Sensous: Essays in Aesthetics*. Trad. Mark S. Roberts y Dennis Gallagher. Atlantic Highlands, NJ: Humanities Press International, 1989.

Eagleton, Terry. *Marxism and Literary Criticism*. Berkeley: University of Los Angeles Press, 1976.

Estévez, Abilio. *Manual de las tentaciones*. La Habana: Editorial Letras Cubanas, 1989.

Fleites-Lear, Marisela y Enrique Patterson. "Teoría y praxis de la revolución cubana." *Nueva sociedad* 123 (1993): 50-64.

Fornet, Ambrosio ed. *Cine, literatura, sociedad*. La Habana: Letras Cubanas, 1982.

Foster, David William. "Directrices del cuento hispanoamericano contemporáneo." *Antología del nuevo cuento hispanoamericano*. Ed. Walter Rela. Montevideo: Ediciones de la Plaza, 1990. 11-26.

Fuss, Diana. *Essentially Speaking: Feminism, Nature and Difference*. New York: Routledge, 1989.

Gorki, Maximo y Zhdanov, A.A. *Literatura, filosofía y marxismo*. Trad. Antonio Encinares P. México, D.F.: Editorial Grijalbo, 1968.

Guerra, Alberto. "Espejo de paciencia." *La gaceta de Cuba* 1 (1995): 43-45.

Gurley, John G. *Challengers to Capitalism: Marx, Stalin, Lenin, and Mao*. New York: Norton, 1979.

Hall, Stuart. "Cultural Identity and Cinematic Representation." *Framework* 36 (1989): 68-81.

Harlow, Barbara. *Resistance Literature*. New York: Methuen, 1987.

Henríquez Lagarde, Manuel. "La literatura no perdona las concesiones: entrevista a Arturo Arango." *El caimán barbudo* 254 (1989): 19.

Heras León, Eduardo. *Los pasos en la hierba*. La Habana: Casa de las Américas, 1970.

_____. "Mateo." *La guerra tuvo seis nombres*. La Habana: UNEAC, 1968. 45-49.

Hernández Catá, Angel. *El ángel de Sodoma*. Madrid: Editorial Mundo Latino, 1928.
Hooks, Bell. "Choosing the Margin as a Space of Radical Openness." *Framework* 36 (1989): 15-23.
Kellner, Douglas. "The Obsolescence of Marxism?." *Whither Marxism*. 22-24 de abril, 1993. Riverside: University of California, 1993.
Lagmanovich, David. *Estructura del cuento hispanoamericano*. Xalapa, Veracruz: Universidad Veracruzana, 1989.
Larguía, Isabel y John Dumoulin. "La mujer en el desarrollo: estrategias y experiencias de la revolución cubana." *Casa de las Américas* 149 (1985): 37-53.
Lastre, Roberto Luis. "El día de cartas." *Letras cubanas* 9 (1988): 96-99.
Lazo, Raimundo. *Historia de la literatura cubana*. México: UNAM, 1974.
Leante, César. "El esposo." *Casa de las Américas* 8 (1961): 54-58.
_____. "Memorias de Vargas Llosa." *Nuevo Herald* [Miami, Fla] 17 de abril 1993: 15A.
Lerner, Marvin. *Sexual Politics in Cuba: Machismo, Homosexualtiy and AIDS*. Boulder: Westview P, 1994.
Lenin, Vladimir I. "Party Organization and Party Literature." *Marxism and Art*. Eds. Berel Lang and Forrest Williams. New York: David McKay Company, 1972. 55-59.
Lezama Lima, José. *Paradiso*. Ed. Cintio Vitier. Nanterre, Francia: Université Paris X, Centre de Recherches LatinoAméricaines, 1988.
López Sacha, Francisco. Prólogo. *La nueva guerra*. Eduardo Heras León. La Habana: Editorial Letras Cubanas, 1989. 5-23.
_____. "Crónica de antaño." *La gaceta de Cuba*. 3 (1995): 47-49.
_____. "El cuento ante la crítica cubana: un fiscal silencioso ante un niño travieso." *La literatura cubana ante la crítica*. Ed. José Rodríguez Feo. La Habana: Ediciones Unión, 1990. 18-26.
_____. Entrevista personal. 15 de junio de 1995.
López, Iraida. "Tres preguntas a Senel Paz." *Areito* 9.35 (1983): 42-44.
Lozano, Angel. "Algo más sobre *Orígenes*." *Linden Lane Magazine* 14.1 (1995): 21.
Medin, Tzvi. *Cuba: the Shaping of the Revolutionary Consciousness*. Trans. Martha Grenzback. Boulder: Lynne Rienner Publishers, 1990.
Montaner, Carlos Alberto. *Informe secreto sobre la revolución cubana*. Madrid: Ediciones Sedmay, 1976.
Montenegro, Carlos. *Hombres sin mujer*. México: Editorial Oasis, 1981.

Mosquera, Gerardo. "Los hijos de Guillermo Tell." *Plural* XX-X.238 (1991): 60-63.
Navarro, Armando. "Incursiones en lo ficticio-fantástico." *Teoría y práxis del cuento en Venezuela*. Monte Avila: Caracas, 1992. 107-128.
Nogueras, Luis Rogelio. "Los pasos en la hierba." *Letras cubanas* 18 (n.d): 202-20.
Ontiveros, José Luis. "Carta a un marxista decepcionado." *Plural* 22-5.257 (1993): 58-59.
Oppenheimer, Andrés. *La hora final de Castro*. Trad. Aníbal Leal. Buenos Aires: Javier Vergara, 1992.
Otero, Lisandro. "Santo y seña: águila negra." *Casa de las Américas* 6 (1961): 69-75.
Padura Fuentes, Leonardo. "El derecho de nacer." *La gaceta de Cuba* marzo-abril (1992): 38-41.
———. "Según pasan los años." *Según pasan los años*. La Habana: Editorial Letras Cubanas, 1989. 7-25.
Paranagua, Paulo Antonio. "Letter From Cuba to an Unfaithful Europe." *Framework* 38/39 (1992): 5-26.
Paz, Senel. "No le digas que la quieres." *El muro y la intemperie*. Ed. Julio Ortega. Hanover: Ediciones el Norte, 1989. 107-19.
———. "*Hasta cierto punto*: continuidad y ruptura." *Alea una retrospectiva crítica*. Ed. Ambrosio Fornet. La Habana: Letras Cubanas, 1987.
———. *El niño aquel*. La Habana: Unión, 1980.
———. *Los muchachos se divierten*. La Habana: Editora Abril, 1989.
———. *El lobo, el bosque y el hombre nuevo*. D.F. México: Era, 1991.
Pérez, Louis A. *Cuba: Between Reform and Revolution*. New York: Oxford UP, 1988.
Pérez Firmat, Gustavo. "Descent into *Paradiso*: A Study of Heaven and Homosexuality." *Hispania* 59 (1976): 247-57.
Pérez Delgado, Nicolás. "Gracias Torcuatico." *Narrativa de la joven Cuba*. Ed. Bernardo Subercaseaux. Santiago de Chile: Editorial el Nascimiento, 1971. 27-31.
Prats Sariol, José. "Cap VIII [de los "Resúmenes críticos de los capítulos"] "Erotismos." *Paradiso*. José Lezama Lima. Ed. Cintio Vitier. Nanterre, Francia: Université Paris X, Centre de Recherches Latino-Américaines, 1988. 661-62.
Pujals, Enrique J. *La obra narrativa de Carlos Montenegro*. Miami: Ediciones Universal, 1981.

Quiroga, José. "Fleshing Out Virgilio Piñera from the Cuban Closet." *¿Entiendes?: Queer Readings, Hispanic Writings*. Eds. Emilie L. Bergman and Paul Julian Smith. Durham: Duke U P, 1995. 168-80.

Randall, Margaret. *Cuban Women Now*. Toronto: The Women's Press, 1974.

Real Academia Española. *Diccionario de la lengua española*. 21 edición. Madrid: Editorial Espasa Calpe, 1992. 396.

Redonet, Salvador. "Para ser lo más breve posible." *Los últimos serán los primeros*. La Habana: Editorial Letras Cubanas; Instituto de Cooperación Iberoamericana; Embajada de España, 1993. 5-31.

_____. "Mi cuento por una pregunta." *La gaceta de Cuba* julio-agosto (1993): 7-10.

Reed, Roger. *The Cultural Revolution in Cuba*. Geneva: Latin American Round Table, 1991.

Reyes, Alfonso. *El deslinde. Apuntes para la teoría literaria*. México: Fondo de Cultura Económica, 1980.

Rimmon-Kenan, Shlomith. *Narrative Fiction: Contemporary Poetics*. London: Methuen, 1983.

Rodríguez Febles, Ulises. "El señor de las tijeras." *Letras cubanas* 16 (1990): 150-151.

Ruhle, Jurgen. "Literature." *Marxism, Communism and Western Society: A Comparative Encyclopedia*. Ed. C.D. Kernig. vol. 5. Ney York: Herder and Herder, 1972.

Sánchez Mejías, Rolando. "La noche del mundo." *Letras cubanas* 8 (198-8): 99-105.

Santamaría, Haydee. "Imagen de un escritor colonizado." *El caimán barbudo* 47 (1971): 16-17.

Santiesteban, Angel. "Sur: latitud 13." *Los últimos serán los primeros*. Ed. Salvador Redonet. La Habana: Editorial Letras Cubanas; Instituto de Cooperación Iberoamericana; Embajada de España, 1993. 171-78.

_____. "Sueño de un día de verano." *Letras cubanas* 14 (1990): 162-69.

Soler Puig, José. "Mercado libre." *Casa de las Américas* 7 (1961): 3-8.

Todorov, Tzvetan. *Introducción a la literatura fantástica*. 2da. ed. Buenos Aires: Editorial Tiempo Contemporáneo, 1974.

Trotsky, Leon. "Proletarian Culture and Art." *Marxism and Art*. Eds. Berel Lang and Forrest Williams. New York: David McKay, 1972. 60-79.

Works Cited

Villanueva, Alfredo. "Carlos Montenegro." *Latin American Writers on Gay and Lesbian Themes: A Bio-Critical Sourcebook*. Ed. David William Foster. Westport, Conn.: Greenwood Press, 1994. 250-51.

Volek, Emil. *Metaestructuralismo*. Caracas: Editorial Fundamentos, 1985.

———. "Análisis e interpretaciones de *El reino de este mundo* y su lugar en la narrativa de Alejo Carpentier. *Unión* 8.1 (1969): 98-118.

Werthein, Silvia y Juan Carlos Volnovich. "Marxismo ¿y/o? feminismo." *Casa de las Américas* 147 (1984): 145-52.